Praise for
Carlton Mellick III

"Easily the craziest, weirdest, strangest, funniest, most obscene writer in America."
—*GOTHIC MAGAZINE*

"Carlton Mellick III has the craziest book titles... and the kinkiest fans!"
—CHRISTOPHER MOORE, author of *The Stupidest Angel*

"If you haven't read Mellick you're not nearly perverse enough for the twenty first century."
—JACK KETCHUM, author of *The Girl Next Door*

"Carlton Mellick III is one of bizarro fiction's most talented practitioners, a virtuoso of the surreal, science fictional tale."
—CORY DOCTOROW, author of *Little Brother*

"Bizarre, twisted, and emotionally raw—Carlton Mellick's fiction is the literary equivalent of putting your brain in a blender."
—BRIAN KEENE, author of *The Rising*

"Carlton Mellick III exemplifies the intelligence and wit that lurks between its lurid covers. In a genre where crude titles are an art in themselves, Mellick is a true artist."
—*THE GUARDIAN*

"Just as Pop had Andy Warhol and Dada Tristan Tzara, the bizarro movement has its very own P. T. Barnum-type practitioner. He's the mutton-chopped author of such books as *Electric Jesus Corpse* and *The Menstruating Mall*, the illustrator, editor, and instructor of all things bizarro, and his name is Carlton Mellick III."
—*DETAILS MAGAZINE*

Also by **Carlton Mellick III**

Satan Burger
Electric Jesus Corpse
Sunset With a Beard (stories)
Razor Wire Pubic Hair
Teeth and Tongue Landscape
The Steel Breakfast Era
The Baby Jesus Butt Plug
Fishy-fleshed
The Menstruating Mall
Ocean of Lard (with Kevin L. Donihe)
Punk Land
Sex and Death in Television Town
Sea of the Patchwork Cats
The Haunted Vagina
Cancer-cute (Avant Punk Army Exclusive)
War Slut
Sausagey Santa
Ugly Heaven
Adolf in Wonderland
Ultra Fuckers
Cybernetrix
The Egg Man
Apeshit
The Faggiest Vampire
The Cannibals of Candyland
Warrior Wolf Women of the Wasteland
The Kobold Wizard's Dildo of Enlightenment +2
Zombies and Shit
Crab Town
The Morbidly Obese Ninja
Barbarian Beast Bitches of the Badlands
Fantastic Orgy (stories)
I Knocked Up Satan's Daughter
Armadillo Fists

THE
HANDSOME
SQUIRM

CARLTON MELLICK III

ERASERHEAD PRESS
PORTLAND, OREGON

ERASERHEAD PRESS
205 NE BRYANT
PORTLAND, OR 97211

WWW.ERASERHEADPRESS.COM

ISBN: 978-1-62105-026-1

Copyright © 2012 by Carlton Mellick III

Cover art copyright © 2012 by Ed Mironiuk
www.edmironiuk.com

Printed in the USA.

AUTHOR'S NOTE

So this is the second book I've written entitled *The Handsome Squirm*. Some of you might remember when my book *I Knocked Up Satan's Daughter* had the same title. Well, the truth is they were originally supposed to be the same book. That's why both stories are about a guy being forced to marry a strange woman he doesn't even know because she's pregnant with his child. But the similarities end there. I had a lot of ideas for this book, but they all just didn't mesh together properly. So I split it into two books: one is a light-hearted bizarro romantic comedy and the other is a semi-perverted tale of absurd horror. The book you're holding in your hands is the perverted one. It's also my tribute to Franz Kafka's *The Trial* and an exploration of a very possible American dystopia.

If you ask me, the scariest dystopian government in the world would be the one which based all of its decisions primarily on making the world a safer place for children. It's human nature to want what's best for the children, so it would be easy for a government to take away our rights if they say it's for their sake.

Worried about Stranger Danger abducting your kid?
No problem! Let's make it illegal for unmarried adult males to go out in public during school hours!

Worried about your child learning naughty words from the neighbors?
No problem! All adults will get censoring devices surgically implanted into their throats so nobody will ever say naughty words ever again!

Worried about children seeing naked people on television, in photos, or anywhere in the world?
No problem! Let's force everyone to get cosmetically altered so that their private parts look permanently pixelated when naked!

That's not too much to ask. We're all willing to make sacrifices for our children, aren't we?

I'm going to guess that this book isn't going to resonate with a lot of people. It's a story for those who have chosen not to have children for the sake of their career. Which really isn't that many people. Deciding against having kids is almost taboo in our culture, especially for a woman or married couple. In Hollywood movies, career-oriented people tend to be portrayed as selfish douchebags who are only redeemed once they have children of their own. For once, I would like to see a movie where a couple decide not to have children and their lives are better for it.

But maybe I'm just an asshole...

So here it is, *The Handsome Squirm*. I hope you enjoy it.

- Carlton Mellick III 3/22/2012 4:32 pm

CHAPTER ONE

The middle of the night and two cops were at my front door, waving a warrant in my face.

"You have to come with us," they said.

Wearing only boxer shorts, I rubbed the gritty sleep from my eyes. Reality wasn't setting in yet. I couldn't quite tell if I was awake or dreaming.

"I don't understand," I told them. "What did I do?"

The cop with sunken gray eyes let out a long irritated sigh, as if just speaking a single sentence was an incredible burden to him. Then he said, "You damn well know what you did."

The metal was cold and sobering when they slapped handcuffs on my wrists.

I said, "I really don't know. What's going on?"

They pushed me into the back of their car and shut the door in my face. They spoke to each other in soft, grumpy voices in the driveway for a few minutes—the red police lights flashing across their uniforms.

I felt incredibly naked and vulnerable in the back seat of the cop car. I didn't have shoes or identification. I really had to piss. My penis was poking out of the flap of my boxer shorts, and with my hands behind my back, there was no way to hide or adjust it. Cum crusted beneath the uncircumcised hood of skin around the head of my penis. I must have had sex with someone that night. With whom, I didn't remember. When the cops got into the front of the car, Gray Eyes looked back at me and shook his head.

"Are you going to tell me why I'm being arrested?" I asked him, leaning over in an attempt to cover my exposed penis with my stomach.

"We don't have to tell you anything," said the cop in the driver's seat. He glared at me through the rearview mirror as

7

he rubbed powdered Cheeto cheese from his blond mustache. "Not anymore, that is."

Ever since the Christian conservative extremists took over the country, laws changed dramatically on a day-to-day basis. Cops had more power than they used to. Churches took a huge percentage out of each person's paycheck whether they attended service or not. Voting was a thing of the past for the majority of the population. And the media had become incredibly restricted. With all of these new conservative laws popping up, I was really curious about what I had done to get arrested. It could have been anything.

I turned to Gray Eyes. I figured if I acted respectfully enough, maybe he would be a little more forthcoming with the information.

"Can you please tell me anyway, sir?" I asked Gray Eyes. "I really have no clue what this is about."

As Blond Mustache pulled out of my driveway, he turned to Gray Eyes. "Just ignore him."

"Please..." I said.

Gray Eyes groaned a when-is-my-shift-going-to-be-over-so-I-can-drink-myself-to-sleep groan.

"You have to know," he said to me. "You received the summons notice two weeks ago, as well as three reminders."

"I'm sorry, sir. I still don't know what you're talking about. What notice?"

"It arrived by mail," he said.

"Who actually checks their mail these days?" I told him. "It's too expensive. I only use email."

Ever since the postal service became privatized, it not only cost money to mail letters and packages it also cost money to receive them. Even if you got junk mail, you had to pay for it. So, like most people who hate getting ripped off, I didn't accept any physical mail anymore no matter who sent it.

"So you really didn't know?" Gray Eyes asked.

I shook my head. "What was the summons about? Was I supposed to appear in court or something?"

The cop shook his head.

"No..." he said. His voice became a little soft, almost concerned. "It was a wedding summons."

"A wedding summons?"

"You were supposed to get married today, but you didn't show up."

I leaned back in the seat, staring at him with confused and crooked eyes. I didn't even care that my penis was hanging out of my underwear anymore.

"What are you talking about? Is this some kind of joke?"

"No joke," he said. "You were summoned to be married and didn't show up, so the bride's family reported the crime. Then a warrant was issued for your arrest."

His words did nothing to relieve my confusion.

"I'm sorry, sir, but this is all very difficult for me to understand. First of all, I was never engaged to be married. Second of all, when did ditching out on your wedding day become a crime?"

"Don't you read newspapers or watch television?" the cop asked. "It's been a law for almost two years now."

Blond Mustache Cop interjected, "Ignorance of the law is no excuse."

"But why?" I asked.

"For the sake of the children, of course."

"I still don't follow you."

"You got a girl pregnant, right?" said Gray Eyes. His tone was like he was speaking to a ten-year-old.

"I did?"

"Yeah, you did. And the new law states that women are no longer allowed to have children out of wedlock. As soon as you knocked that girl up, you lost the right to be a bachelor. The pregnancy was reported, the DNA was tested, and by law the two of you were supposed to get married today. By leaving your pregnant bride at the altar you committed a very serious crime."

"Don't bother explaining it to him," Blond Mustache Cop said to Gray Eyes. "There's no way he didn't know about that

9

law. Everyone knows about that law."

I didn't know what to say. Anger, shock, and panic overwhelmed my system. I was no longer confused, because I believed them. This sounded exactly like the kind of law the new government would pass.

The new government overthrew the old one for a single reason: they believed family values should be upheld above everything else, including an individual's rights. Under the new government, the only people allowed to vote were home-owning families with three or more children. All movies and television programs that weren't family-friendly were banned. Owning or selling pornography was a federal offense. To cut down on drunk driving, all bars had a two-drink maximum. Even swearing in public carried a hundred dollar fine.

I knew that abortion had become illegal. I also knew that divorce was illegal, if kids were involved. But I had no idea it had become illegal to have children out of wedlock. So when a couple got pregnant, not only must they keep the child, but by law they must also get married and stay married whether they liked each other or not. Failing to raise children properly in a wholesome family environment had become a very serious offense.

"So what's going to happen to me?" I asked the cops. "What's the punishment for skipping out on a wedding date?"

The two cops looked at each other. I could tell they were happy they weren't in my shoes. Gray Eyes looked back at me.

"Eighteen years is the minimum sentence," the cop said.

"Eighteen years! Are you fucking kidding me?"

Blond Mustache Cop gave me the evil eye for saying the F-word in front of him, but the cops let it slide. They decided not to fine me for it.

"You should have just married her," said Gray Eyes. "Trust me, eighteen years as a family man is far better than eighteen or more years in prison, even if you don't get along with your wife."

"But I didn't even know about it," I said. "I don't even

know who the woman is that I got pregnant."

The cop looked through his papers for a couple of minutes.

"Dokura Silivasi," said the cop. "Ring any bells?"

I repeated the name over and over in my head, trying to put the name to a face.

"Not at all," I said.

I wasn't expecting to recognize the name, though. I was a swinger. I slept with a lot of women. I rarely remembered any of their names. Still, I wished I could figure out who she was.

"You wouldn't happen to know when she was impregnated, would you?" I asked.

The cop went through his papers. "The pregnancy was reported three weeks ago. She was about six weeks pregnant at the time. So you had to have had your encounter with her around two months ago."

"Two months ago?" I looked out the window, thinking about it.

Off the top of my head, I could think of nearly a dozen possible women. But I was sure there were even more that I couldn't recall at all.

"What does she look like?" I asked. "Do you have a picture of her?"

The cop with the sunken gray eyes shook his head.

Then the cop with the blond mustache said, "It doesn't matter what she looks like. You missed your chance to do the right thing and now you're going to jail for a long time."

"But I didn't know about any of this until now. If I knew, I probably would have been at the ceremony."

Or at least have gotten out of the country before I could be arrested.

"Too bad," said Blond Mustache. "It's up to the judge now."

"The day isn't technically over yet," I said. "If I still get married before the end of the day you can't arrest me, right?"

They didn't respond.

"Right?" I repeated.

"It's too late," said Blond Mustache.

"But it's still the date of the wedding. Would you arrest a guy just because a wedding was delayed?"

"You missed your chance," said Blond Mustache. "It's fifty minutes to midnight."

Gray Eyes let out a long sigh at his partner. "No, he's right."

Then he turned to me. "Technically we are supposed to give you one last chance to marry the girl before we take you in."

"Why the heck did you tell him that?" Blond Mustache said to his partner. "I don't want to go all the way out into Usagi country in the middle of the night."

Gray Eyes turned to me. "I can probably get the charges dropped if you're willing to marry the girl tonight. Is that what you want?"

I nodded my head. I didn't know what else to do.

"Are you sure? If you're only going to use this as an opportunity to escape, things are going to be a lot worse for you. I'll make sure of that."

"I'm sure," I said. "I'd much rather be a father than a convict."

Gray Eyes nodded his head and called it in.

CHAPTER TWO

The cops didn't talk to me for a while after they called it in. They turned the car around and got on the interstate.

"So is it okay?" I finally asked them. "Am I getting married or going to jail?"

Gray Eyes looked back at me. "The wedding is still in process. They said if we get you there within the hour all charges will be dropped and you can still get married."

"Wait, it's still happening? Why is the wedding still going on at this hour?"

Gray Eyes didn't respond.

They drove me out of town. After about thirty miles, they got off at an exit in the middle of nowhere and headed down a small forest road. Then they turned down an even smaller road. No sign of houses or civilization anywhere. As soon as they took a dirt road, I began to get a little worried.

"Where are we going?" I asked them.

They didn't respond.

Part of me wondered if they were taking me out into the woods to kill me. I came to the realization that it was possible they were lying about the wedding and the new law. Cops now have the power to do whatever they want with little consequence. They could have just been playing a game with me. I was half-expecting at any minute they'd pull over, take me out of the car and then tell me to run into the woods in my boxers and handcuffs. They'd give me a ten minute head-start and then hunt me down for sport.

But they didn't stop. They just kept driving deeper into the woods.

"There's nothing out here," I told them. "Are you guys trying to mess with my head or something?"

"We're taking you to your wedding," said Gray Eyes. "It's

in Usagi country."

I didn't know what he was talking about.

Blond Mustache looked at me in the rearview mirror. "I don't envy you, kid. Of all the women you could've knocked up you chose an Usagi chick."

"What's an Usagi?" I asked.

They turned around and stared at me for a while. Blond Mustache didn't even care that he was driving with his eyes off the road.

"You don't know the Usagi?" Blond Mustache asked. "Even though you knocked one of them up?" He turned his eyes back to the road. "Man, you have no idea what you're getting yourself into."

Gray Eyes looked at me. "I'm not really surprised you haven't heard of them. Very few people outside of this area have ever heard of the Usagi. Heck, even people around here know very little about them. They don't really allow outsiders into their communities."

"Are they like a cult or something?"

"Well, it's more of a subculture than a cult. Think of them as Quakers or gypsies. They have their own customs, their own beliefs. They are mostly shut off from the outside world."

"They also have their own language," said Blond Mustache. "It's a cross between..." He turned to Gray Eyes. "What are they a cross between again?"

Gray Eyes said, "Their language and ethnicity is a mix of several cultures, but they are mostly a cross between Romanian and Japanese."

"Well, I've never heard anything about them before," I said, "and I've lived in this part of the country my whole life."

"They've been here for a few decades now. I believe the culture itself is a couple of centuries old, with small pockets of communities spread throughout Asia and Eastern Europe."

I shook my head. "It's crazy I never heard of them."

Blond Mustache said, "What's really crazy is that you've actually slept with one. How could you even do that? Those people creep me out."

I was beginning to get worried about what I was getting myself into. I asked, "What's so creepy about them?"

Blond Mustache said, "It's their eyes, especially. Their eyes are unnatural in color—a bright neon blue. And their hair is so black it looks like oil. Plus they have absolutely no sense of humor whatsoever. They don't even smile. Ever."

"Those are just urban legends," said Gray Eyes, shaking his head at me.

"And they wear human bones as jewelry," Blond Mustache said. "And the women have weird mutant nipples."

"What do you mean by mutant nipples?"

"I don't know. They're just supposed to be weird somehow. Like they're bright purple or really long or something like that."

I didn't remember sleeping with any woman strange enough to match his description. I've slept with a ton of weird chicks in the past. In fact, I've always been a magnet for weird chicks. But none of them were as strange as the Usagi women he described.

"Ignore him," Gray Eyes told me. "Those are just myths."

"What does Usagi mean anyway?" I asked.

"It means bunny."

"Why are they called that?"

Blond Mustache chuckled. "Because they breed like rabbits."

At first I thought he was just joking, but then Gray Eyes nodded his head in agreement.

Blond Mustache said, "If you're marrying an Usagi woman, prepare to have a dozen more kids after the first one. They're all about increasing their numbers."

Gray Eyes glared at the driver. "Quit scaring him. I'm going to be pissed if we drove him all the way out here only to have him change his mind at the last minute."

Blond Mustache responded, "He's probably better off locked in a cell for a couple of decades than marrying an Usagi."

"Just shut up about it. He'll be fine."

Then I noticed my penis shriveling up and hiding itself back inside the flap of my boxer shorts.

CHAPTER THREE

The forest opened up to a small village. Pinecone-shaped houses with black spiky roofs, somewhat reminiscent in style of buildings from eighteenth-century Japan, lined the dirt road. We drove slowly, gawking at the Usagi homes. All of the windows were dark and empty, as if nobody lived in them.

"What the heck's up with these houses?" Blond Mustache asked before I got a chance to. "Do people actually live in them?"

"Yeah, I heard they have a unique style of architecture," Gray Eyes said. "But I've never actually seen it before."

Barbed-wire sculptures of dog-headed people guarded the outside of each building. A long row of large animal cages on wheels identical to those of a traveling circus sat empty, rust forming on the iron bars. The whole place reminded me of a long-abandoned carnival.

"This place gives me the creeps," said Blond Mustache. "I hate the Usagi."

Gray Eyes agreed. "Let's just get this over with as soon as possible so we can get the heck out of here."

I looked down at my boxer shorts.

"What am I supposed to do about clothes?" I asked them. "I'm still in my underwear."

"Not our problem," said Blond Mustache.

"I can't just show up to my wedding in boxer shorts," I said.

"You'll be fine," said Gray Eyes, brushing me off. "I'm sure they'll dress you up nice before the ceremony."

At the end of the road, in the dead center of town, stood a church. It was the largest building in the village, but instead of the spiky Japanese style it was more castle-like. A gothic fortress. Dim candlelight emanated from stained-glass windows. It was the only lighting in the entire area besides the headlights of the cop car and the light of the moon hovering overhead.

The car pulled up to the building. Blond Mustache kept the engine running. He wasn't planning on stepping one foot out of the vehicle. We waited in the car for a few minutes for somebody to come out and greet us.

"So you say they're like Quakers?" I asked the cops.

"Not exactly."

"But they are a bunch of religious nuts, right? If their community revolves around this church they must be some kind of Jesus freaks."

"In all honesty, I really have no idea what they're like," Gray Eyes said, nervously scanning my arrest warrant as if procrastinating the task of handing me over to the Usagi. "As I said, they're a very private people."

An older woman emerged from the building and approached the cop car. The shiny black dress she wore looked like it had been designed for a fetish masquerade ball. Her massive cleavage bulged out of the top. Slits up the sides of the dress revealed her waist and thighs, exposing thigh-high fishnet stockings. The shoulders of the dress had long black tendrils dangling down the sides. As she moved, the tendrils seemed to come to life, squirming against her cleavage like jellyfish.

All three of us in the car were surprised to see a woman in her late fifties dressed in such an outfit, especially for a wedding. She stepped seductively across the dirt road on ten-inch stilettos, one foot in front of the other like a model going down a runway.

"What's up with her?" Blond Mustache said. "Is that a Halloween costume?"

Seeing the woman's outfit made me relax a little. It was an unusual dress for a wedding, but at least it proved the Usagi were not the insanely conservative religious nuts I was expecting them to be.

"Wait here," Gray Eyes said.

He stepped out of the car. Blond Mustache and I watched from inside the vehicle as the police officer approached the woman. She had no expression on her face as she spoke, showing no emotion, like a machine. Gray Eyes kept his arms crossed and left a comfortable distance between them, yet he couldn't take his eyes off of the woman's cleavage as he spoke to her.

"What's the name of the girl I'm supposed to marry again?" I asked Blond Mustache.

"Silivasi," he said.

"What about her first name?"

Blond Mustache shrugged.

When Gray Eyes finished speaking to the woman, he opened the door and pulled me out of the car. I found myself face-to-face with the pale-skinned woman as Gray Eyes unlocked my handcuffs. I had lost a lot of weight recently so my boxer shorts were extra loose. They began to slide down, revealing the crack of my ass in the back and the tip of my pubic hair in the front.

The woman wasn't the slightest bit bothered by my nudity. She looked me up and down, like a judge in a dog show. She examined the area of my crotch for an uncomfortable amount of time, as if trying to estimate the size of my penis behind my underwear. Once the cuffs were off of my wrists, I pulled my boxer shorts up and held them there. She looked me in the eyes and licked her bottom lip with a quick strike of her tongue.

When I saw her eyes, I realized that the cops were right about the Usagi appearance. They were such a bright blue that they appeared to glow in the dark.

I turned my attention back to the police officer.

"We're leaving you in Mrs. Silivasi's care," Gray Eyes said to me.

I looked at Mrs. Silivasi. She was the mother of the bride. My future mother-in-law.

"Do whatever she tells you to do," continued Gray Eyes. "She's taking custody of you until the ceremony is over and the papers are signed. Don't make us come back here."

I nodded at the officer. Then he patted me on the shoulder and got back into the cop car. The officers drove out of the village as fast as they could go in reverse, leaving me in a cloud of dust. Then I was alone, in front of the church, in the dark, with the strange woman.

After an uncomfortable length of silence, she said, "You're five hours late."

She had a thick accent. Not the Japanese or Romanian accent I was expecting. It was closer to a Swedish accent.

"I'm sorry," I said. "I only found out about it an hour ago."

"I don't need excuses," she said. "I just need a husband for my daughter."

I nodded.

As she led me toward the church, she said, "Dokura has been waiting her whole life for this day. She has put so much time and effort into making everything absolutely perfect down to the finest detail. When you didn't show up today, it nearly ended her. She wouldn't let anyone leave their seats, hoping beyond hope that you'd actually arrive."

"As I said, I'm sorr—"

"Just don't ruin it anymore for her."

"I won't," I said. Then I looked down at my boxer shorts. "Do you have anything for me to wear? The cops picked me up while I was sleeping."

"Your suit is inside," she said, and then led me through a side entrance into the church.

CHAPTER FOUR

Inside the church, I found myself in a reception hall. It was large and empty. For the most part, it looked like a normal reception area before a wedding: tables dressed in white tablecloths with black folded napkins, sparkling silverware, and glimmering candles. But there was something not quite right about it. The emptiness mixed with dim candlelight gave the room a sad and lonely feeling. It seemed more like a wake than a wedding. The centerpieces on the tables were not made of flowers, but instead were wild mushrooms—bright, colorful, poisonous mushrooms.

"Can I see Dokura?" I asked the woman.

I wanted to know who I was getting married to before seeing her at the altar. I really hoped my bride was one of the more attractive women I'd slept with. There was at least one woman I could think of who was so hideous that jail time might have been the preferred option.

"Not before the wedding."

I nodded. Part of me wanted to ask her to describe Dokura to me, but I really didn't want to let on that I had no recollection of ever meeting her daughter. I was already in enough trouble with these people.

"The ceremony will begin shortly," she said. "You'll see her soon enough."

In the candlelight, the woman's eyes were not quite as bright as they were outside, yet her short black hair was twice as shiny. It was like vinyl and matched the texture of her dress.

I looked down to discover a necklace around the woman's neck. The cops had said the Usagi wear jewelry made out of human bones. It wasn't a myth. On a silver chain, dangling between the woman's breasts, was a bone the size of a human finger. The woman licked her lips when she saw me staring at her necklace. She thought I was looking at her cleavage.

"We need to get you prepared for the ceremony," she said. "Everyone's waiting for you."

I nodded.

"I need to use the bathroom first," I said.

She pointed at a door on the side of the room. "Go through there. Dokura's sisters will dress you."

"They'll dress me? I said I need to use the bathroom."

She nodded. "They'll help you with that as well."

It seemed odd to me that she was having her daughters help me get dressed and use the bathroom. Were I female, it might have made more sense. I decided not to argue with her. I had to go to the bathroom way too badly to ask any more questions.

"I'll be waiting here for you when you're ready," she said, as I rushed toward the side door.

The next room was much smaller than the reception hall. It was a private lounge, full of couches and tables. A candelabra in the center of the room was the only light source.

Lounging on the couches were seven women. All of them wore dresses similar to Mrs. Silivasi's fetish ball costume, yet even more revealing. The backs were cut out and I could clearly see their nipples through the thin fabric covering their breasts.

When they noticed me, all of them stood at attention. An eighth woman crawled out from under the dress of another. I had no idea what she was doing under there, but as she wiped moisture from her mouth it made me wonder if she was giving the other woman oral sex.

They didn't say a word to me, just stood there stiffly. I felt a little awkward having a group of women staring at me in my boxer shorts.

I assumed they were Dokura's bridesmaids, because they were wearing matching dresses. Not only did their dresses match, but all eight of the women looked exactly alike. They were about the same height and weight, and close to the same age. Their long black hair was also all the same length, stretching down to the centers of their backs.

"I'm looking for Dokura's sisters," I said.

"We're her sisters," one of them said. Her accent was even thicker than the mother's.

"All of you?"

"All of us," they said in unison.

The cops were right about the Usagi having a lot of children. Eight daughters? Plus Dokura, that made nine. They sure did breed a lot. I really hoped Dokura didn't want to have more than the one child with me. Fathering one I could probably handle, but fathering nine would be another story.

Because the sisters all looked alike, I assumed Dokura would also share their physical appearance. But they were unfamiliar to me. I didn't remember sleeping with anyone who looked remotely similar to them. Perhaps their sister was adopted or maybe only their half-sister.

"I guess you're supposed to help me get dressed," I told them. "But it's okay. I can dress myself."

One of them said, "It's tradition for the bride's sisters to dress the groom for her."

Another said, "It's our job to make sure you look appetizing enough for her."

They all licked their lips seductively at the word appetizing. If I didn't know any better I would have thought they were planning to feed me to the bride that night. If the mother was wearing a human finger bone as jewelry, I wouldn't put it past them to also practice cannibalism. None of these women were wearing human bone jewelry, but the way they were looking at me with their neon blue eyes did give me the impression that they were a bunch of radioactive mutant cannibals.

"Shall we begin?" they asked in unison.

"I have to use the bathroom first," I told them.

One of them stepped forward, the one who had moisture on her lips. She kneeled down in front of me.

"Here," she said. Then she opened her mouth as wide as she could.

I had no idea what she was doing. It was as if she wanted me to urinate in her mouth.

"So..." I said, my voice a little shaky. "Where is the bathroom?"

They all just stared at me with their normal expressionless faces. The girl with the opened mouth closed her eyes tight, her tongue wiggling gently inside her mouth. I stepped away and headed toward a door on the other side of the room. They followed me with their ghostly eyes.

"Is it through here?" I asked, my hand on the doorknob.

They didn't respond. The girl on her knees still had her mouth open, still had her eyes closed. As I opened the door, a gust of wind blew into the room and raised their dresses, exposing their asses through tight mesh panties. They did nothing to cover themselves, just stared at me with icy eyes.

I stepped into the bathroom and closed the door. It was the size of an airplane lavatory with no sink or shower, just a toilet and a roll of toilet paper. The only source of light came from moonlight shining through the open window to my left. The window covered the entire wall from floor to ceiling. It was large enough that I could have probably stepped out into the cold forest if I wanted. Thoughts of escape rushed through my head.

I pulled my penis out of my boxer shorts and relieved myself. Looking down into the toilet, I realized it wasn't a real toilet. It was more like an outhouse. Not only did the place have no electricity, it also didn't have indoor plumbing. The sound of my urine splashing against the bottom of the pit made a high-pitched echo, as if it were splashing against something meaty.

It felt good to finally empty my bladder. One of the worst parts about getting arrested was that cops never let you use the bathroom no matter how bad you had to go, no matter how long they planned to detain you. It seemed like a form of torture.

As I pulled up my underwear, I saw something moving down inside of the toilet. Just for a split second. I couldn't quite tell if it was just my imagination or not, but I could've sworn that down inside of the toilet there was a pair of glowing blue eyes staring up at me.

When I returned to the lounge, all eight women were crowded around the bathroom door, waiting for me.

"Are you ready?" they asked in unison.

I nodded my head.

One of them took me by the wrist and pulled me into the center of their circle. Then she kneeled down and pulled off my underwear. As her long black hair brushed against the shaft of my penis, I felt an erection begin to form. The woman on her knees looked up to see it pointing at her. I tried to think of something else, something that would turn me off, but being undressed by a group of beautiful women made it incredibly difficult. Before the erection could fade, the woman on her knees took my penis in her hand and stroked it a few times to make it even more erect. Then the other women squeezed in closer and grabbed at me, rubbing my body with scented oils.

"Is this normal?" I asked them.

They didn't respond. Sixteen hands massaged my flesh from all sides, loosening my muscles and kneading tension out of places I didn't even realize were tense. They continued for several minutes. Eventually, they didn't even seem like eight people anymore. They were just one creature with many hands.

"You Usagi have some strange customs," I said.

One of them hushed me, and then she massaged my penis with the scented oil before the erection could fade. It almost seemed as if the identical sisters were about to gang-bang me right then and there, like something out of a horny teenager's wet dream, but as soon as the thought entered my brain they all stopped.

As they took their hands away, my skin tingled as if they were still touching me somehow. Then they wrapped my erect penis in a ribbon. Each one of them took a turn wrapping it and with each binding they chanted a phrase in their language. I guessed it was like some kind of Usagi blessing. After my penis was completely covered, the ribbon was tied in a bow, just below the penis head.

"Why did you wrap my penis like that?" I asked.

"It is our custom," one of them said.

Another continued, "to wrap the groom's penis as a present for the bride."

"Dokura will open this gift on her wedding night," said another.

"A gift from us to her."

They finished each other's sentences as if they shared the same brain. All of them stared at me with their creepy glowing eyes and blank expressions. The Usagi really were as strange as the cops had described. The only thing I thought the cops were wrong about was the weirdness of the Usagi women's nipples. I could clearly see their nipples through their nearly-transparent dresses, and they looked perfectly natural. Nothing mutant about them at all.

"I see..." I said to them.

"Now for the suit," they said.

As a team, the women dressed me in my wedding suit. The clothes were very nice, but obviously handmade. All of the Usagi clothing seemed to be custom-made. The white shirt they buttoned onto me was very similar to a normal tuxedo shirt but quite a bit frillier. The suit coat was much different from a standard tuxedo. The tails were so long they almost touched the ground. The shoulders had the same black tendrils as the women's dresses, and even when wearing the coat myself, the tendrils seemed to come to life and curl around my chest and into my armpits. The tie was a ridiculous abomination of black tentacles hanging from my neck. And the cufflinks were big white squishy balls reminiscent of testicles.

It was an unusual outfit but I didn't mind wearing it. That is, until they pulled my pants on. The suit pants were not pants at all. They were more like a pair of black ballerina tights. Not only that, but they were incredibly transparent. Everyone at the wedding was going to be able to see the large gift-wrapped bulge in my pants.

After putting a pair of shiny black shoes on my feet, one of them stood up and leaned close to my lips.

"There you go," she said, inches away from my face. "Now you look delicious."

Then she licked my face from the bottom of my chin to the top of my forehead.

At that point, I had to admit it: if I was going to marry into a weird cult, at least it was a weird kinky sex cult.

CHAPTER FIVE

When the women escorted me out of the lounge back into the reception hall, I saw my future mother-in-law holding a top hat and a black cane. She approached me and put the hat on my head and the black cane in my right hand. In my left hand, she put a black rose.

"For Dokura," she said.

I looked down at the rose to see specks of blood forming in my palm. The stem still had its thorns. For some reason, I didn't feel a thing.

Mrs. Silivasi looked me up and down, re-evaluating me in my new suit.

"You look very...tasty," she said. "You'll do just fine."

More thoughts of cannibalism crossed my mind as the woman kissed my cheek. Then she grabbed my crotch, squeezing my penis as casually as testing the ripeness of a cantaloupe.

"Keep it hard," she said to me. "You don't want the wrapping to come undone. Okay?"

I didn't respond. Getting fondled by my future mother-in-law had left me speechless.

"Are you ready?" she asked.

I nodded my head slowly. Then I realized what was going on and shook my head.

"I don't know, am I ready?" I said. "There wasn't a rehearsal. I have no idea what I'm supposed to do."

Behind me, the eight sisters rubbed the back of my suit as if trying to wipe off cat hair.

"There's no time for rehearsal," she said. "The reverend will tell you everything you need to know."

"Do I need a ring or anything like that?"

"We don't use rings in our ceremonies."

"Then what do I give her?" I asked. "Is it a wrist-tying kind of thing?"

"No," she said. "What you will be giving her is far more personal."

"What is that?" I asked her.

The woman reached up to her neck and grabbed her necklace, holding the finger bone in the palm of her hand for me to get a closer look.

"You'll give her your ring finger," she said.

For a split second, I thought she was joking. But her radiating eyes quickly told me that she was dead serious. I tried to back away, but a wall of women prevented me from moving.

"You're going to take my finger off?" I asked. "So she can wear the bone on a necklace?"

The mother nodded.

"I'm not going to do that!"

She glared at me for a moment.

"Would you prefer to go to prison?" she asked. "It's the only way Dokura will marry someone. If you love her then you should be willing to give a part of yourself to her."

How could I love her? I didn't even know who she was.

"Why can't we just do rings?" I asked.

"She's not marrying a ring," the mother said. "She doesn't want a ring. She is marrying flesh, and so she wants a commitment of flesh."

"Marriage is about sacrifice," the sisters said behind me, in unison.

"You really want your daughter to lose a finger over this?" I asked.

"Dokura won't be giving you her finger," she said. "She will be giving you something else."

"What's that?"

"Her brand," she said. "A mold of her love was made and during the ceremony it will be branded to your chest, over your heart."

"What!" I cried. "I lose a finger and she gets to burn me? How is that fair?"

"You're going to be her husband," she said. "Enduring a little pain for the ceremony is a very small sacrifice to make."

I looked over at the exit and then glanced back at the women standing behind me. I wanted to get the heck out of there and try to flee to Canada. But the second the thought entered my head, several women standing behind me grabbed my shoulders and held me in place as if they had read my mind.

"The oils my daughters rubbed into your skin should help numb some of the pain," the mother said. "You won't have to worry."

I was more worried about losing a finger than feeling the pain.

"We mustn't waste any more time," the mother said. "You've kept Dokura waiting long enough."

I nodded a nervous awkward nod.

She took my arm in hers and positioned us in front of the double-doors leading into the church. The ceremony was about to begin.

"Are you ready to do the handsome squirm?" she asked me.

"The handsome squirm?"

She squeezed my arm and said, "That's what we call it when a groom walks down the aisle on his wedding day."

I nodded my head at her, too nervous to speak.

Then she escorted me through the doors and into the squirm.

CHAPTER SIX

The audience was so quiet that I could hear my own breath echoing through the chapel as Mrs. Silivasi escorted me down the aisle. There was no music. Dead silence. Three hundred glowing blue eyes fixated on me. All of their faces were devoid of emotion. Every Usagi in the room wore elegant yet provocative attire. It really felt like a fetish ball. Some women wore even more revealing clothes than Dokura's sisters. Even the elderly women dressed as if they were on their way to an orgy. More than a few people didn't seem to be wearing any clothes at all.

As I walked, their eyes followed me. I stared straight ahead, holding the black rose out like a candle as I stepped slowly toward the altar. I was surprised to see a large marble crucifix at the front of the room. These people didn't strike me as Christian. The cops made it seem as if they had their own unique religion. But I wasn't sure if their faith was a comfort or a cause for alarm.

The eight identical sisters followed us down the aisle, two-by-two. A reverend stood by the altar—an old man in a long purple robe. I was thankful that at least he was not wearing fetish attire.

Mrs. Silivasi grabbed my penis and yanked on it. I nearly yelped.

"You're becoming flaccid," she whispered. Though she was whispering, everyone could clearly hear her through the silence. "Don't you dare ruin this for my daughter."

But the anxiety made it impossible to keep an erection. She squeezed tighter. Still nothing. She pulled me by my member all the way up the aisle. My penis didn't become erect again until the girl walking behind me opened her mouth over my shoulder and licked the back of my neck and around my ear.

When I got to the front of the room, Mrs. Silivasi released

my penis, turned me around to face the audience, and then sat down in the front row. The eight sisters came forward and separated, four of them stood on my right side, the other four standing on my left. They were both the bridesmaids and the groomsmen for this ceremony.

There was an uncomfortable length of silence as I stood up there facing the audience. I noticed my erection was pointing out at the crowd. Their eyes seemed focused on the bulge, which caused me to go soft again. The girl on my left, where the best man should have been, caressed the back of my thigh and then gripped my ass. She wasn't just a groomsman. She was also my fluffer. Her job was to keep me turned on throughout the ceremony.

Violin music began to play and the audience turned their attention to the back of the room. Two obese men dressed in nothing but black and white body paint stepped through the double-doors and shuffled to the side of the room. One of them played a violin in such a fast, wild manner that it sounded more like the squeals of a vampire bat. The other man played a cello, striking at the chords as if he were ringing a funeral bell. The music of the two instruments was supposed to prepare the audience for the coming of the beautiful bride. But all it sounded like to me was impending doom.

I was anxious to see the bride. I really wanted to know who she actually was. The ceremony, where my finger was to be removed, I was not impatient for. A part of me was hoping that I still had a chance of escaping the finger-amputation. Perhaps Dokura would have pity on me and just do a simple wrist-tying ritual at the last minute.

The double-doors flew open and long spider-legs stepped into the room. It wasn't the bride. It was two women on stilts, coming down the aisle toward me, wearing long white silk gowns. Black and white swirls were painted on their faces and naked breasts, which dangled out of rips in their clothing. They moved like creeping insects on their stilt legs, shifting and swaying to the rhythm of the violin music, tossing white flower petals into the air to create a path to the altar.

As they reached the front of the aisle, they joined hands and tied the bottoms of their gowns together while kissing each other with forked tongues. When they separated, the fabric of their connected gowns created a hammock filled with white flower petals. Raising it like a canopy over my head, the stilt walkers and the hammock of flowers became a living arbor for the ceremony.

While staring up at the women on stilts towering over me, I could see the bottoms of their breasts above my head. For some reason, this stiffened my erection. The fluffer groped me from behind and then pulled my face down into her own breasts, as if she were jealous that the stilt walkers were doing a better job keeping me aroused.

"She's about to come," the fluffer whispered into my ear, moving my face away from her breasts into the direction of the double-doors. "Feast your eyes on the beauty of your bride."

CHAPTER SEVEN

Everyone in the room stood from their seats and prepared themselves for the bride's introduction. Those who were wearing hats removed them from their heads.

She emerged like a flower in full bloom. She sucked all of the candlelight out of the room and radiated it back at us from her white gown. The dress was all I could really make out from where I stood. All I saw was a wide, white, billowing gown with a long train. The top of her low-cut bodice had the same tendrils as her mother's and sisters' dresses, but these were white and thick like octopus tentacles. She held a bouquet of white flowers in her hands.

A veil covered her face, so I couldn't tell what she looked like outside of her body shape and the long black hair behind her shoulders. From what I could tell, she looked identical to her sisters.

As she came closer, I realized that the front of her dress ended at the mid-point, revealing her body from the waist down. She wore garters with ripped thigh-high stockings. Her mesh panties were also exposed and a stripe of pubic hair was clearly visible through the underwear. It was as if her dress was designed to be wedding ceremony on the top and wedding night on the bottom.

She didn't get any more familiar the closer she came. I wondered if I was ever going to remember who she was. Then a thought crossed my mind: what if this was all a mistake? What if they got my name mixed up in the DNA lab and some other guy knocked up this girl? I would have gotten screwed for nothing. Maybe I'd even get my finger removed for nothing.

But as the bride approached me, her bright blue eyes glowed at me through the veil. She definitely recognized me. Her eyes locked on mine as she stalked up the aisle toward me, like a predator coming for her prey.

Once she arrived directly in front of me, I still didn't recognize her. I could make out most of her face through the veil. She was just a stranger to whom I was about to dedicate the rest of my life.

The music came to an abrupt stop. I handed the bride the black rose that her mother had given me. When she accepted it, she bowed to me. I bowed back. Then she took her place below the stilt walkers' canopy by my side. We faced the reverend and the ceremony began.

The reverend spoke to me. His words came out in such a thick accent that I thought he was speaking Usagi tongue. I had no idea what he said. When I didn't respond, my fluffer tapped my shoulder to give my attention to the old man. Then the reverend repeated himself. He held out his hand to me. I still had no idea what he was talking about.

"Hand him your cane," my fluffer whispered in my ear.

I handed him my cane.

The old man said some more gibberish that I couldn't understand in the slightest. Then he raised my cane and unscrewed the top, revealing a hidden compartment. He pulled out a vial of fluid, opened it up, and poured it into a hand-painted chalice. Then he handed the chalice back to me.

"Drink it," my fluffer whispered.

I looked down at the fluid. It was yellow and thick. It smelled sulfuric. Looking over at my bride, I saw her haunting blue eyes watching me, as if excited for me to drink. I looked back at the congregation. Mrs. Silivasi was glaring at me.

Her eyes told me, "You're ruining everything."

When I sipped from the chalice, the liquid fizzed against my lips. It tasted of peaches, dandelions, and ammonia. The reverend took it from my hands and gave it to my bride, who guzzled down the entire chalice through a hole in her veil.

It was some kind of toast for the beginning of the ceremony. Immediately, a burning sensation filled my body. The fluid must have been some kind of strong Usagi liquor. My muscles quickly loosened, relaxed, yet my mind became sharp and clear.

My fluffer slipped her hand into my coat and caressed my inner thigh, but it wasn't necessary. I was fully erect. It was almost as if the drink was an aphrodisiac.

The reverend then gave a speech to the congregation. This time I believe it was spoken in the Usagi language. I couldn't understand a single syllable. Because I couldn't understand the speech, my mind began to wander. I dazed off, wondering about how they were going to remove my finger. The alcohol had my brain swimming in euphoria. By the time the reverend finished his speech, my mind was a million miles away.

"Face your bride," my fluffer whispered, jabbing at my kidneys with her index finger.

I looked over and saw my bride facing me. Then I turned to her. She held out her hands and I took them in mine. We stared into each other's eyes. Her neon irises seemed to be glowing brighter and brighter. They looked almost demonic behind the veil. The white tendrils curling out of her dress squirmed against her body like tentacles. I couldn't tell if the dress was actually alive or if it was just the effects of the strange alcohol.

The reverend spoke to us. This part of the ceremony seemed as if we were about to exchange vows. When the reverend stopped speaking, there was a long silence. All eyes were on me. Mrs. Silivasi looked as if she was about to get out of her seat and rip my throat out.

I figured I was supposed to repeat what the reverend had asked me to vow, but because I didn't understand what words he was speaking I had no idea what to say.

My fluffer saved me again.

"Repeat these vows," she whispered in my ear.

As she whispered the vows to me, I said them aloud.

"You are the woman I will give myself to," I said to my bride. "My love will be yours and only yours, my flesh will be yours and only yours, my soul will be yours and only yours. We will become one flesh so that our offspring will become many."

The vows were ridiculous, but I said them anyway. I didn't

have another choice. Though, as ridiculous as they might have been, my bride and all of the Usagi around me appeared to have tears in their eyes. Then the reverend asked me another question, translated by the woman behind me.

"Will you prove your commitment with an offering of flesh?" she whispered. Then she said, "Say I will."

"I will," I said.

There was a pause.

"Now offer her your flesh," my fluffer whispered.

I didn't know what she meant.

"Give her your left ring finger," she clarified.

I looked down at my finger, wondering if I was supposed to cut it off myself. The reverend didn't have any kind of finger-chopping device I could see.

"How?" I whispered to the fluffer.

She whispered back, "Put it through the hole."

I looked around for a hole, but had no idea what she was talking about. At first I thought there might have been some kind of finger-guillotine on the altar, but there was nothing like that. When I looked up at my bride, I noticed that her mouth was open. That's when I found the hole where I was supposed to put my finger. It was the hole in her veil, in front of her mouth. Dokura was supposed to acquire my finger by biting it off.

I could feel my knees getting weak. Mrs. Silivasi said nothing about having my finger bitten off. Having it amputated at all was bad enough, but removing it with teeth seemed about the most painful method possible.

"Stick it through the hole in her veil," the fluffer whispered.

"I know," I whispered back.

"Then do it," she said.

I looked in Dokura's blue eyes. She hadn't expressed a lot of emotion before, but now I could clearly see a look of excitement behind those eyes. I tried to look pathetic, show her that I really didn't want to go through with this aspect of the ceremony, hoping that she would agree to come up with an alternative to the finger-biting ritual. But the expression on her face didn't change. She wanted my finger.

My left hand was shaking as I lifted it toward my bride's veil. Her breaths quickened when she saw my hand coming toward her face. She leaned in closer, widening her mouth. Drool seeped through her veil. A desperate moan oozed out of her lungs as I extended my ring finger. I could feel her hot breath against my knuckles.

Perhaps it was the alcohol or perhaps it was because I felt put on the spot, but the next thing I knew I was pushing my ring finger through the hole of my bride's white veil.

"Put it all the way in," my fluffer whispered into my ear, caressing my backside. "As far as it can go."

I felt the warmth of her drool-soaked tongue as I slid my finger all the way into her mouth. Dokura stared deep into my eyes as she closed her lips. I braced myself for pain, but she didn't bite right away. First, she sucked on my finger, tasting it, savoring the experience. Then she closed her eyes and pressed her jaws together with all of her strength.

My fluffer grabbed me by the shoulders as my shrieks filled the chapel. The pain hadn't been numbed at all. My body thrashed around, trying to yank myself out of her mouth. But her jaws had too good a hold on it. When I threw my arm around, her head just moved with it. She would not let go.

All eight of Dokura's sisters jumped me and held me in place. Then they began to suck on my neck and grab at my penis, trying to keep me aroused while enduring the pain. It took several minutes before my bride popped the finger out of the joint and chiseled through the veins and tendons. Blood gushed from her lips, splashing across her white wedding dress and pooling on the floor.

When she was done, my hand fell away from her face with a snap. I looked down at the empty space between my pinky and middle finger, screaming as a red fountain gushed out. The sisters wrapped my hand in a tourniquet to stop the bleeding, as Dokura removed the finger from her mouth and handed it to the reverend.

"Stop screaming," my fluffer said to me. "It will upset your bride."

I tried to hold in the pain as the old man strung my finger like a bead onto a silver chain. He presented it to Dokura, placing it around her neck. She held the still-warm finger in her hand as if gripping a rabbit's foot for luck.

Once I calmed down and was ready to continue with the ceremony, we faced each other again. The sisters returned to their positions, careful not to slip on my blood in their stilettos. Dokura released my severed finger and let it dangle in her cleavage, then took my quivering hands in hers. It was her turn to say her vows.

The reverend placed a small stove on the altar and ignited it with a candle. He raised a branding iron and handed it to Dokura. As he told her the vows she would repeat, my bride held the branding iron within the flame.

When Dokura gave her vows, I heard her voice for the first time. It was a soft yet somewhat deep voice—the voice of a woman with confidence, the kind of woman who always got what she wanted. As I heard her vows, I realized that she wasn't quite making the same commitment to me that I had made to her.

"I am the woman you will give yourself to," she told me. "Your love will be mine and only mine, your flesh will be mine and only mine, your soul will be mine and only mine. We will become one flesh so that our offspring will become many."

Then the reverend said something to Dokura along the lines of: "Will you prove your commitment with a mark of your love?"

Dokura said, "I will."

When the branding iron was hot enough to burn my flesh, she pointed it at me.

"Now you will be marked with a symbol of your bride's love," the fluffer whispered in my ear. "Do not cry out. You must accept her love with joy."

Then the fluffer ripped open my shirt, baring my chest to the heated metal. As the iron came toward me, I learned exactly what they meant by a symbol of my bride's love. The iron was a mold of Dokura's vagina.

Her eyes were locked on mine as she burned an imprint of her cunt on my chest. I tried to smile as I smelled my own cooking flesh. When she took the iron away, I looked down at the brand. It reminded me of a kiss mark, only the lip prints were clearly vaginal.

She handed the branding iron back to the reverend, who spoke a few passages in Usagi tongue. The last line he spoke was translated by my fluffer.

She whispered, "He said I pronounce you husband and wife. May your coupling bear much fruit."

Then she licked my earlobe.

"Now kiss your bride."

The fluffer released me from her groping hands and pushed me toward my new wife. I raised Dokura's veil from her face, and before kissing her I examined her features, trying to remember where the heck I originally met the woman. She just looked like another of her sisters. Perhaps she might have been a little different, but I couldn't tell them apart.

As I kissed her, the guests jingled tiny bells like applause. Then the stilt walkers released the canopy and dozens of white flower petals rained over our heads.

After the audience stopped ringing the bells, Dokura didn't stop kissing me. She only got more into it, sucking my tongue into her mouth and caressing my legs. She wrapped the sides of her wedding dress around me and shoved our crotches together.

I could taste my blood in her mouth as she furiously made out with me in front of everyone. Her family watched with emotionless expressions. They just sat quietly in their seats as the loud smacking noises of our tongues echoed through the chapel.

CHAPTER EIGHT

The musicians burst into another noisy song. This one seemed like it was trying to be more joyous and festive. But it just sounded like the background score to a movie about deranged killers stabbing women in alleyways.

Dokura couldn't keep her hands off me as we walked back down the aisle away from the altar. The sisters, the stilt walkers, and my new mother-in-law followed behind us. We formed a row outside of the reception hall. As the guests left their seats and exited the main chamber, they congratulated us one at a time by giving Dokura an open-mouthed kiss. Even the elderly women, who seemed to be her grandmothers, kissed my bride with their tongues. Some of them kissed her for several minutes. Some of them grabbed her breasts. Some of the younger women even sucked on my severed finger hanging from Dokura's neck.

I felt disgusted, embarrassed, and even a little jealous for some reason. But these people had their weird customs and I decided it would be best not to say anything about them. Most of the guests did not kiss me. They just kissed the branded mark on my chest and said, "Welcome to the family." Their saliva made the wound sting with pain, but it did not seem too creepy until I remembered that they were actually kissing an imprint of Dokura's vagina.

Dokura's sisters were the most aggressive when congratulating the bride. They all attacked her at once with their lips, tongues, and teeth. They nearly ripped her out of her gown right in front of everyone. But it wasn't sexy. It seemed as though they kissed her with anger and vengeance, as if they were jealous that Dokura had gotten married before them. One of them sucked on my severed finger so deeply that she nearly swallowed it.

When it was my turn, the sisters were even more aggressive.

They nearly picked me up off the ground and ran away with me, as they viciously attacked my neck and face with their tongues. But they did this not out of anger, more like out of desperation and sexual frustration. They were gentle with my gift-wrapped penis, but each took a turn stroking it. Part of me thought this was a wet dream come true, but it really wasn't as great as I would have fantasized. It was more embarrassing and awkward than pleasurable.

When they were finished, one of the sisters, I believe the one who was my fluffer, said to me, "You're Dokura's property now," as she straightened my suit and flattened my frazzled hair with her palm. "We're not allowed near you ever again."

She kissed my burned chest softly. Then I watched her ten inch heels as they stepped carefully out of the room toward the reception area. When I looked back, I found myself face to face with Mrs. Silivasi.

"You were satisfactory," she said to me. She looked back at Dokura who was making out with a tiny old man. "She is very happy."

I didn't know how the mother could tell Dokura was happy. The girl had not smiled once since I'd seen her. She was just a cold, finger-biting, sex-fueled machine. When the little old man finished kissing my bride, the mother brought him over to me.

"This is Dokura's uncle, Stefan," said Mrs. Silivasi.

"Good to meet you," I said to him.

"Yes, yes," he said to me. "Congratulations. You'll fill up our beautiful little Dokura quite nicely."

I didn't understand what he meant by that, but assumed he meant something incredibly inappropriate. The incest that went on in this cult was just far too perverted, even for me. I might have been a swinger who had quite a lot of depraved sex with multiple partners at the same time, but these people were crossing a line.

Before I could wave the man away, he wrapped his arms around my hips and kissed the burn on my chest. He spent a long time kissing it, sucking and licking the burn, causing me to cringe in both pain and disgust.

41

A groaning noise came from Uncle Stefan. When I looked down, I noticed that he was licking the vagina-shaped brand as if he was giving it oral sex. He was really getting into it—his eyes closed, biting on the vaginal lips, twirling the tip of his tongue against the clit. The creepy old son of a bitch was imagining the vagina-shaped burn was Dokura's real vagina.

I looked up at Mrs. Silivasi with a distressed expression, begging her for help. But she just looked at me with blue demon eyes, an emotionless reptile. So I looked down, at our feet. There was something peculiar there that grabbed my attention. It was Uncle Stefan's shadow. Although the man was short and thin, he had the shadow of a morbidly obese person.

"What is wrong with your shadow?" I asked Stefan, hoping the question would get him away from my naked chest.

He froze in his place when he heard my question.

"It is huge," I said. "You're thin, but you have the shadow of a fat person."

Stefan removed his lips from my wound and wiped the saliva from his face. Then he bowed to me and ran out of the room.

Mrs. Silivasi glared at me.

"Why did you say that?" she asked me.

"What do you mean?" I said. "I was just curious. Didn't his shadow look strange to you?"

"That was incredibly rude," she said. "Stefan's shadow has a weight problem. He is very sensitive about it."

"His shadow is overweight?" I asked.

"We don't talk about it around him," she said. "Don't do it again."

"Okay...I won't."

"Good," she said. Then she pulled me to her. "Now let me kiss my beautiful new son-in-law."

Instead of kissing me, she pulled my face into her cleavage and rubbed her breasts against my cheeks.

"You're going to give my daughter beautiful children," she said, as she squeezed my ass and tongued my ear.

CHAPTER NINE

I had many weird sexual encounters in my life, but nothing had prepared me for that moment. As I made out with my mother-in-law, in front of my bride, on my wedding day, I began to wonder if I had originally met Dokura at some kind of depraved sex party. She definitely seemed like the type to attend such events. But her face still didn't ring any bells.

There was one orgy I had been to around the time that Dokura would have been impregnated. I had sex with four women that night, but their faces weren't clear in my memory. I tried to retrace my steps...

That orgy was actually a memorable one. Not because of the women I had slept with, but because of the protestors. It was the first orgy I had been to that allowed anti-orgy activists.

When I entered the room, I found myself behind a blockade of angry religious people. One of them held a sign in my face that read, "Group sex is for sinners." Another sign read, "Swinger = Satan."

I pushed my way through the crowd and found myself stopped by a police officer.

"Are you here for the party or the protesting?" the cop asked. The cop had a blond mustache. It probably wasn't the same cop with the blond mustache that drove me to my Usagi wedding, but their mustaches were identical.

"I'm here for the party," I told the policeman.

He let out a sigh and had me fill out a form. Then he checked my identification.

"What's this all about?" I asked him.

"New protocol," he said. "Making sure you're of legal age and not already married. Adultery is illegal now, as I'm sure you know."

"It is? When did that happen?"

The cop called in my driver's license and ran a background check on me.

"We also need to keep track of who attends these events and make note of which sexual partners you consort with. Your employer will also need to be notified."

"Is all of this necessary?" I asked him.

"Of course," he said. "It's the law."

Then the cop let me pass.

As I went toward the wet bar, I wondered what my boss was going to say once he got the report of my orgy activities. He was a very conservative family man and I knew he would not be happy one bit. Luckily, he knew I was irreplaceable. I was the most valuable editor at his publishing company. Perhaps I didn't have seniority over a lot of the other editors, but I made the press a shitload of money because I could do something that none of the other editors could do: I could turn new unmarketable writers into money-making machines. Perhaps the older editors had all the top writers—the bestsellers, the celebrity memoirs, the movie tie-in novels. But any editor could make money publishing books that already had large built-in fan bases.

It took a very special kind of editor to build a fan base for an unknown. My belief was that all fiction was commercial. Even the most anti-commercial pretentious high-art novels had commercial potential. You just had to figure out a way to package the book so that it would appeal to the anti-commercial pretentious high-art audience.

I also knew something that very few people in the publishing industry understood: there's nothing more marketable than uniqueness. If a writer was doing something that nobody else was doing, then there would be no one to compete with. Readers who wanted that kind of book would only be able to buy from that particular author. It was called cornering the market.

Succeeding in the publishing world was not about riding trends. It was about creating them. And more than anyone in the industry, I knew how to find the trend-setting writers.

When I got to the wet bar, I poured myself a beer.

"Good luck getting a buzz off of that," said a voice behind me.

It was Dave. A lawyer friend I knew through the industry. He was the one who got me into swinging in the first place.

"What's that?" I asked him.

He pointed at the beer. "The damned new liquor laws. Nothing over three percent alcohol can be sold anymore. You're more likely to get full than drunk with that shit."

Then Dave bit into a corndog. He was naked in front of me, walking casually through the kitchen as if it were his own home. I'd seen him more in the nude than I'd seen him with clothes on, so this wasn't all that unusual of an occurrence for me.

"What's with the protestors?" I asked him.

He glanced toward the crowd of Christians in the entryway.

"New law. Didn't you hear?"

"No," I said.

Dave's incredibly large penis was erect and pointing at me. I tried to keep my distance from it.

"These days we need a permit to throw a swinger party," he said. "They must be monitored by law enforcement and the public has the right to protest."

"What about freedom of privacy?" I asked.

"A thing of the past," Dave said, and chuckled.

A glob of mustard fell on his penis. He wiped it up with the tip of his corndog and took another bite before saying, "You need to get out more. This is old news."

"I don't pay attention to the news," I told him.

"You work in the media," Dave said. "It's your job to follow the news."

"I work in fiction," I told him. "It's my job to keep my head in the clouds."

Dave shrugged.

Two women approached us. They were naked with fake tans and breast implants. Not my kind of girls. I'd take small breasts over implants any day.

"You guys want to go?" they asked us.

The one with the curly blond hair grabbed Dave's penis and stroked it in front of me.

"You're all ready to go aren't you?" she asked him. I couldn't tell if she was thirty or fifty.

Dave continued eating his corndog as if nothing was happening.

"You're not ready to go at all are you?" the other girl asked me, the one with short blond hair.

"I just got here," I told them.

"Let's get these clothes off of you, then," she said, pulling off my shirt.

I looked around the room, then asked, "Where's the condom bowl?"

The girls giggled at me.

"There's no condom bowl," said the short-haired woman. "Condoms have been outlawed."

"What?" I asked.

"It's true," Dave said, casually chewing on his corndog as the curly blond licked the shaft of his penis.

"Why would they outlaw condoms?"

"They didn't want teenagers having sex."

"That doesn't make any sense."

"Well, that's what happens when moralistic idiots take power."

"So we're just going to have unsafe sex?"

"Don't worry," said the short-haired girl as she removed the last of my clothing. "We're on the pill."

"They didn't outlaw the pill?" I asked.

"Not yet," she said.

"What about STDs?" I asked.

"The cop wouldn't have let you in if you had any STDs on your record," Dave said.

He was now fucking the blonde from behind. Even though he was fucking her, he was still facing me and casually eating his corndog.

"It doesn't matter anyway," Dave said. "All of this is going to be illegal eventually. I wouldn't be surprised if they didn't just outlaw sex altogether and make us reproduce through artificial insemination from now on."

"That would be too insane, even for them," I said.

The short haired girl aimed my penis at her crotch and said, "Better get fuckin' while you still can."

As I entered her, the policeman walked by. He stopped in front of us, looking us up and down, holding up his clipboard like a food inspector. He took down our names, keeping record of who was having sex with who, then moved on.

The short-haired woman looked behind her shoulder at me and giggled.

"That was kind of hot," she said.

I shook my head at her. It was not the slightest bit hot.

The two women faced the protestors, as Dave and I fucked them from behind.

"Look what you're missing, bible-thumpers," the girls yelled at them, groping their fake breasts and licking their nipples.

"You sluts will burn in hell!" the protestors yelled.

But that only turned the women on more. For some reason, they got off on having an angry mob in front of them during sex.

"So anyway," Dave said, "about that contract you sent over the other day..."

Dave always had the habit of talking to me while we were fucking girls in the same room together. It was always something mundane, like sports or the weather or some boring case he was working on. He was like one of those guys who constantly talked to you while you're standing at the urinals together. But instead of talking to me while urinating, Dave talked to me while fucking.

"Think I can have a few more days to look it over?" he asked me.

"Yeah, sure," I said, trying to stay focused.

It was difficult enough having sex in front of the protestors. I didn't need to have a conversation with Dave at the same time. He could tell I wasn't enjoying myself. He knew I wasn't too attracted to the woman I was doing it with.

"Want to switch?" he asked, nodding toward our girls.

"Sure," I said.

The girls switched partners without hesitation.

These were two of the four women that I slept with that night. I pretty much remembered what they looked like—Dokura definitely wasn't either of them. There were two others that I slept with, but I couldn't quite remember their appearance. I knew that I had a threesome with them later that night. One of them sat on my face as I gave her oral sex. I didn't remember what she looked like, but I remembered she was Puerto Rican or something like that. So she definitely wasn't Dokura.

There was another girl riding on top of me, though. It was possible that she was Dokura. Unlike the two blondes with breast implants, these girls didn't tell me whether or not they were on the pill. It was possible this was the woman I impregnated. I just assumed all the women were using some kind of birth control.

But I didn't remember actually seeing this woman. My face was buried between the Puerto Rican girl's legs most of the time. The girl had joined in after I started giving oral. It was possible that I never even saw the face of the woman who was fucking me. It definitely could have been Dokura. The two women switched positions with each other a few times, but I still didn't see the woman's face. When she lowered her crotch onto my lips, all I saw was a strip of black pubic hair and smooth white thighs.

I decided it must have been Dokura. It was the only option that made any sense to me.

CHAPTER TEN

Dokura and I didn't really speak at all for the next few hours after the wedding. She held my hand as tightly as she could and wouldn't let go. But she said nothing. In fact, nobody really said anything to anyone.

Everyone crowded into the reception hall and sat around the tables. Dokura and I were at the head table, sitting by ourselves in the center of the room. We were served plates of food: cocktail wieners, cheese balls, sardines, cherry tomatoes, and seaweed crackers. All a bunch of crap. Luckily, there was plenty of honey wine. I drank as much of it as I possibly could.

It was as if we were on stage as we ate. Everyone just stared at us, sitting at their tables in silence. I felt uncomfortable being in the spotlight, but even more uncomfortable sitting next to my bride. She was a total stranger to me, a stranger wearing a blood-splattered wedding dress and my finger hanging from her neck.

I looked around the room at all of the quiet, mechanical people as they ate. It seemed the women outnumbered the men ten-to-one. Almost half of the children were male, but there were not as many men my age. Besides the reverend and Uncle Stefan, there didn't seem to be any males over the age of fifty.

When I locked eyes with Mrs. Silivasi, she stood from her seat and came to me.

"Is there a problem?" she asked me.

"No, of course not." I broke eye contact with her. "I was just curious. How come there aren't many men in your community?"

Mrs. Silivasi blinked. "We encourage our men to become fathers."

I wondered why she avoided my question. Instead of repeating myself, I let my eyes wander the room, looking back at all the people who were staring at me.

"What are you looking for?" Mrs. Silivasi asked.

I shook my head. "Nothing."

"You appear to be looking for an escape," she said.

"Escape?" Dokura asked.

I looked at my bride and shook my head. "No, of course not. My eyes were just wandering."

"We do not like wandering eyes," said Mrs. Silivasi.

"I'm sorry. I did not mean anything by it."

"If you were thinking of escape you should know that it would be of no use," she said. "You're already bound to Dokura, committed to her. Your opportunity to escape has passed."

"I wasn't trying to escape."

"You must stay by her side at all times."

"Of course I will," I said, and took Dokura's hand as a sign of dedication.

"You'll never leave her sight. Not for a second."

"Well, I can't promise every single second."

"Yes, every single second."

"Even when I go to the bathroom? Even when I have to go to work?"

"You won't go to work," she said. "The only work you have to do from now on is be a father."

I snickered a bit and looked around the room to see everyone staring at us. Dokura's emotionless face pointed at me, not responding. Then I looked back at Mrs. Silivasi's ghostly stare. She was dead serious.

"But I've got an important job to do. I'm not going to just quit."

"There is no job more important than becoming a father."

"Look," I said, raising my voice. The alcohol mixed with adrenaline gave me some courage. "I was legally obligated to marry your daughter and be a father to her child, which I have agreed to do and will fulfill my side of this deal. But I do not have to give up my career. I had a life before this wedding and I don't plan on throwing it all away."

Mrs. Silivasi stared at me for an uncomfortable amount of time.

Then she said, "Your old life is over. You must make great sacrifices for the sake of your children. That's what it means to be a father."

"You expect me to just give all of that up and live here in this little village for the rest of my life?"

"Exactly," said Mrs. Silivasi.

Then she walked away. I wanted to tell her she could go to hell, but I figured that wouldn't be the best thing to say at the moment. I decided to let it go. I knew they could not just keep me here against my will for the rest of my life. The government would be on my side. They would want me to take my wife and child away from this weird sex cult. They would want me to keep my job as an editor to provide for my family.

I ate in silence for a while. Mrs. Silivasi's words rolled around in my head. The more I thought about it, the angrier her words made me. So I tried to drown my thoughts in honey wine.

Whenever I looked over at Dokura, she would stare at me. In my drunkenness and pain and boredom, I decided to stare back. I tried to see how long I could stare at her before she broke eye contact, but she wouldn't break eye contact. She kept her eyes locked on mine, not eating or drinking. It was as if she wanted us to continue staring at each other for the rest of the night. She showed no emotion, but she seemed to be receiving an incredible amount of pleasure from this experience. It was like she was getting to know me, telepathically. I finally broke the stare in order to take a drink.

"Are you enjoying yourself?" I asked her, trying to start a conversation. I had to do so in a whispering tone. I didn't want everyone in the room listening to us.

She nodded in response.

"Do you like my finger?" I said, pointing at her bloody necklace. I could tell I was getting pretty drunk by asking such a question.

She looked down at her necklace.

"I hope so," I said. "It's yours now."

As a response, she grasped my finger on her necklace and inhaled deeply.

"I'll keep it with me, always," she said to me. Her voice was loud, not in a whisper at all. Everyone could clearly hear her. She wanted them to hear.

She stared at me, as if trying to get me to stare back at her again. But I was bored with just staring.

"I feel as if we hardly know each other," I whispered to her. "We only met briefly before tonight."

She didn't say anything, just staring at me.

"Tell me about yourself," I said. "What's it like being an Usagi?"

She cocked her head slightly. Even though it was a slight motion, it seemed as if she was telling me that she found my questions annoying. She didn't want to talk. She just wanted us to look at each other. So I stopped talking and as we sat there, eating the crappy cold food, and staring each other down. The more we gazed into each other's eyes, the deeper Dokura breathed. It was as if the experience was turning her on.

Before I was done eating, Dokura pulled me out of my seat and brought me onto the dance floor. She went to the corner of the room and put a cassette tape into a boombox (circa 1979). Then she pushed play.

The music began with a tacky drum-machine beat. She kept her back to me as she began to dance, shaking her butt from side to side with the electronic drum beat. When she turned to face me, the guitars and bass tracks exploded into song. It sounded like a cheesy 80s Russian rock band, but with a Japanese female vocalist who sang in such a high-pitched off-key manner that at first I thought somebody was strangling a cat.

Dokura danced toward me, wiggling her hips and sliding her thighs together as she strutted across the dance floor in an attempt to be seductive. Her dance seemed choreographed, as if she had been practicing for days to get it just right for this very moment, yet at the same time her dance was so dorky-looking that I couldn't help but wonder if it wasn't the first time she had ever attempted to dance in her life.

But she had an incredibly serious look on her face, staring at me with seductive eyes as she swayed her belly to the tacky rock music. I didn't know I was supposed to join her in the dance until she grabbed me by the hands and pulled me closer. When she grasped my injured hand, I cringed until she let it go.

I didn't need to do much to dance with her. Her wiggling body pressed against me gave the illusion that I was following her moves. Everyone watched us blankly, like they were watching grass grow.

After a couple of minutes, Dokura spread her legs and began grinding my left thigh as she danced. She kissed my neck and squeezed my ass. Although she seemed to have no desire to express herself emotionally, she had no problem expressing herself sexually.

I hoped the song would end soon, but it didn't. It just kept going. We didn't stop dancing the awkward dance until the tape ran out. Then we stood there on the dance floor in silence for a while, with everyone watching us. Eventually, we returned to our seats and the second I sat down I guzzled half a bottle of honey wine in one gulp.

Nothing happened for the rest of the reception. There was no wedding cake. No party. When it was over, everyone just stood up and walked out, without saying anything to each other.

"We can go to our home now," Dokura said to me.

I nodded at her. My head was spinning with the amount of alcohol I had consumed.

"I want to open my wedding gift," she said.

Then she patted my crotch. To my surprise, I was somehow still erect.

CHAPTER ELEVEN

Outside the chapel, snow covered the ground and rooftops in a blanket of white. The cold air bit at my burned chest. I buttoned the suit coat. But because I was wearing a thin pair of tights instead of pants, there was nothing I could do to keep my legs and ass from freezing. Dokura, however, did not seem cold at all. The lower half of her body was just as exposed to the freezing temperature as mine, but the cold didn't faze her in the slightest.

We walked in silence for a while, stepping down the snowy moonlit road. Dokura held my gift-wrapped penis in her hand as we walked, pulling me along as if I were a dog on a leash. She exhibited so much confidence and dominant energy as she stepped effortlessly through the snow on her ten inch heels. That combined with her fetish outfit, she reminded me of a dominatrix—the kind of dominatrix I used to be able to hire when they were still legal. But there was something about her that was different from a regular dominatrix. She wasn't putting on a show. There was something very informal about her authority. She pulled me along the road by my penis as casually as if she were holding my hand while on a stroll through the park.

A gust of wind chilled the backs of my legs. Had she not been holding my penis, I would have immediately lost my erection.

"It's freezing out here," I said to her.

She looked back at me with glowing blue eyes.

"Don't worry," she said to me, locking eyes with mine. She wasn't looking where she was going as she walked. It seemed as if she didn't need to. "It will be warm inside of me."

We arrived at a small building near the edge of the forest, most of it shadowed by the nearby trees. Dim candlelight flickered through the small, circular, porthole-like windows.

"Our new home," Dokura said.

"It's lovely," I told her, my voice shaking.

I had no idea what else to say. I really couldn't see what it looked like outside of the windows and the spiky black roof rising out of the shadows.

"My family built it for us just last week," she said.

"Their wedding present to us?"

She nodded. "It is Usagi custom for the bride and groom to spend their wedding night in a house built specifically for them. The house symbolizes the birth of our union. It is our nest. We will mate here, birth many children, and make it our home for the rest of our lives."

As she said that, I realized that the Usagi really were from a completely different world than I was. I had no desire to birth many children with Dokura, nor live in this house for the rest of my life. They were a community of psychopaths.

"What's it like inside?" I asked.

"I don't know," she said. "I haven't seen inside yet. It's a surprise for us both."

"Okay, then," I said, excited to get out of the cold. "Let's check it out."

The interior of the house was about the size of a studio apartment—just one large room, plus a closet, plus a bathroom that lacked modern plumbing. The walls were decorated in black and red ribbon. Dozens of candles illuminated the room with a soft glowing light. White flower petals covered the wooden floor like carpeting.

The bed in the center of the room was also covered in flower petals. It took up most of the space, as if the whole house revolved around the bed. It was circular and twice the width of my king-sized bed at home. It looked twice as comfortable as well.

"Come into our nest," Dokura said, pulling me to the bed.

I thought she was trying to be cute by calling our bed a nest, but as I crawled onto it I realized the bed really was a nest. Beneath the silk sheets, the bed was just a mound of soft hay. Like a bird's nest or maybe a rat's nest. It was incredibly comfortable, but still...the Usagi really sleep in nests?

"Why do they call you Usagi?" I asked Dokura.

"It means bunny," she replied, as she crawled into the nest with me.

"That's what I heard," I said. "But why bunny?"

Dokura removed the veil from her head and tossed it onto the floor. Then she lifted up the side of her hair.

"Because of our ears," she said. "They look kind of like bunny ears."

When I examined more carefully, I realized that the black handful of hair she held up was a long floppy ear, like the ear of a rabbit. But the ear wasn't covered in rabbit fur. It was coated in human hair, which blended so perfectly with the rest of her hair that I never would have noticed they were ears if she hadn't pointed them out to me.

"Serious?" I reached out my hand and felt her ears. They were real. "Do all Usagi have ears like this?"

"Most of them," Dokura said.

I thought back to all the Usagi I met at our wedding. They could have had ears like this hidden in their hair, but I never would have noticed.

"How is that possible?" I asked.

"I don't know. It happened to my family ages ago, long before my people came to this country."

"It's like a mutation?"

"Yeah," she said.

Once I believed her, I realized that the Usagi weren't just freaks in the cultural sense. They were genuine mutant freaks as well.

"It's just like our eyes," she said. "And our nipples."

"Wait..." I looked down at her breasts. I could see her

nipples through her clothing. They didn't look freakish to me. "Your nipples?"

"Yeah," she said. "Our nipples are different from yours."

She stood up from the bed and removed her wedding gown, exposing her naked breasts to me. Her breasts seemed normal. The nipples on her breasts also seemed normal. Not just normal, but perfect. But then I saw marks going down her torso.

Dokura took my hand and rubbed it down her breasts, then down her ribs and belly, over the small circular marks. At first I thought they were imprints left by her corset. But, as my fingers touched them, they became erect. Each circle puckered and swelled. She had a total of ten extra nipples. Five on each side, lined up with the real nipple on each breast. I'd known a lot of people who had extra nipples. But I'd never seen anything like this before.

After using my hand to rub her row of nipples a second time, Dokura began to breathe heavily. She took the palm of my hand and squeezed one of her breasts with it. She looked down at my penis, then gazed up at me with her glowing blue eyes.

"Can I open my present now?" she asked me.

I looked down at my gift-wrapped penis, then back up at her.

"Okay," I told her.

As she pulled the ribbon to release my penis from its wrapping, I examined Dokura's extra nipples more carefully. From a distance they didn't look like nipples. They looked more like birthmarks. Or maybe tattoos.

Then it hit me. I remembered when I first met this woman. I remembered when we had sex. As she grabbed my penis, my skin began to crawl. I couldn't believe I hadn't thought about it sooner. It was as if my memory had blocked it out. Of course it was her. I'd never had a stranger sexual encounter in all my life.

CHAPTER TWELVE

It happened at a rest stop along a desolate highway, late at night, in the middle of nowhere. I was heading home from a cabin that I had rented to get some extra work done over the weekend. Whenever my writers would get blocked up, I always told them they needed to find a cabin or a hotel far away from everything, where there was no internet or television or anything interesting to do for miles around, then do nothing but write and write until their projects were done. I used the same method when doing editing work. If I ever got behind on my work, I always got a hotel for a day or two. But this time I decided to try a cabin. In a cabin, it almost felt like a vacation even though I did nothing but edit the whole time.

However, this was an exceptionally frustrating weekend. The author I was editing required a lot of work. The first thing you learn as an editor is that every book ever written, no matter how brilliant, is flawed. Every bestseller is flawed, every classic masterpiece of literature is flawed—every book ever published could have been better in one way or another. As an editor, it was my job to get rid of as many flaws as possible, even if I had to pretty much rewrite the entire book myself. This was basically what I had to do that weekend in the cabin in the woods—rewrite a whole fucking book.

At most, a writer is only capable or willing to rework about thirty percent of his novel after it is complete. This particular book needed to be at least sixty percent reworked. Those changes were my responsibility. The publisher didn't give a fuck. He didn't even read the books he published. He just wanted me to turn in the project by the deadline, no matter how much work was required.

"And it better damned sell," the publisher would always say.

After finally completing the last draft of the manuscript that Sunday night, I celebrated with a bottle of whiskey. It was only fifteen percent alcohol, due to the new liquor laws, but after chugging the entire bottle, I was pretty drunk. Then I took a nap, woke up, packed, and hit the road by three a.m. I had a five hour drive ahead of me and needed to get to work on time.

I was pretty liquored-up still, even after the nap. And worse, I was delirious from lack of sleep. The problem with a weekend-long work marathon was that I never got any sleep.

There weren't any cars on the road, thankfully. My driving was terrible, swerving back and forth between the lanes. I could hardly keep my eyes open. When I got to the first rest stop, I decided I had to get off the road. I parked my car and took a quick nap. Then I did a dozen jumping jacks and bought some cold drinks from a vending machine. There weren't any other cars at the rest stop. Not a single car drove by on the highway while I was there.

In the bathroom, my eyes began to droop again as I stood at the urinal. I had no idea how I was going to wake myself up enough to drive. After I zipped up my pants, I decided I would have to call in sick that day. I knew that I could still email over the final manuscript to my boss, which was all he needed from me that day anyway.

When I turned around, a woman appeared out of nowhere. She must have been standing in the back of the room, watching me the whole time. She had a feral look about her. She wore a long raggedy shirt like a dress, cuts and scrapes on her legs and arms. I thought she had to have been some kind of escaped mental patient. Or some crazed junky.

"Are you okay?" I asked her. "What are you doing in here?"

She didn't speak, just stared at me through the long black hair in her face.

I walked toward the exit, but she moved in front of me, blocking my path. Looking over her shoulder into the parking lot, there still weren't any more cars out there. I had no idea how she got there. We were all alone.

"Do you need a ride somewhere?" I said. "I can give you a ride."

She nodded slightly at that. At least, I thought it was a nod. "Come on," I said. "Let's go."

As I tried to get through the door, she still wouldn't move from my path. Trying to push my way through, she leaned into my face and sniffed at my neck, inhaling my sweat. When I looked her in the eyes, she grabbed me by the pants and pulled me back into the bathroom, into one of the stalls. My mind was so hazy at that point I thought it was all a dream. I no longer thought she was a stranded junky or escaped mental patient, I thought she was some kind of ghost, like the ones from Japanese horror movies. The ghost of a dead hitchhiker who was raped and killed on that stretch of highway. Now she was getting her revenge by raping and killing men at this rest stop when they were alone in the middle of the night.

Those were the thoughts I had as the woman removed my clothes and proceeded to fuck me right there in the bathroom stall. She never spoke a word to me, just stared at me with her ghostly eyes. As we made love, I noticed the tattoos she had on her torso. Small coffee-colored circles lining her ribs and stomach. They didn't seem unusual to me at the time. I never would have suspected they were extra nipples.

When she had an orgasm, her mouth dropped open and her eyes lit up in surprise. It was as if she'd never had an orgasm before in her life and wasn't expecting the sensation. She nearly strangled me while she came for what seemed like several minutes. Then I came into her. It was unlike any orgasm I'd ever had before. It lasted longer than usual, for one, but it also felt different; as if my soul were being sucked out of me.

After we finished, I was exhausted. Lying against the bathroom wall with the woman on top of me, I no longer had the energy to move. I passed out right there.

I closed my eyes for what seemed like half a minute. When I opened them, the girl was gone. Vanished. I pulled up my pants and went outside. The parking lot was still empty. The highway was still silent. There wasn't a soul in sight. I almost decided that the girl really was a ghost until I felt my back pocket and realized my wallet was missing.

"That bitch," I said, when I realized that the woman definitely stole my wallet.

I no longer thought she was a ghost. I thought she was just some crazy chick that wanted to rob me—a junky drifter, too high to realize what she was doing to me back there. Looking around at the surrounding forest, I wondered if she was camping out nearby. I had no idea she was actually an Usagi, living in a strange cult-like community somewhere in those woods. We had unprotected sex, so I began to worry that I might have caught some kind of disease off her. Little did I know I had impregnated her that night.

I went back to my car and just passed out. There was no way I could get back on the road. There was no way I could even call in sick at work. I lay in the driver's seat for hours, going in and out of sleep. In my dreams, I had visions of that ghost girl. She kept crawling into my car with me to make love to me again, every couple of hours or so. I was too out of it to really know whether that was real or a hallucination.

CHAPTER THIRTEEN

As Dokura fucked me slowly in our nest, it seemed as if I were making love to a completely different woman than the crazed junky ghost girl from the highway rest stop. This Dokura was more elegant and mature. She seemed a lot taller, meatier, and healthier. I wouldn't necessarily call the Usagi civilized, but she did seem more civilized than the feral version of herself I had encountered.

The pain from my missing finger died away as I came close to orgasm. She put all of her weight on my shoulders, staring at me, holding me down as if she were worried I would try to escape before we finished. When she came, a weird noise rose out of her—a squeaky, inhuman rumbling. Her vaginal lips tightened and vibrated around my penis in a way I had never felt before. Then I ejaculated into her, the biggest orgasm I had ever had, gushing like a geyser.

As I came, Dokura licked her lips and gazed deeper into my eyes. She held me in place, locking our crotches together.

"It's never been like this," I said to her, between moans.

While I continued coming inside of her, I experienced a split second of joy. Perhaps marrying Dokura wouldn't be such a bad thing. Maybe having tons of amazing sex in a love nest for the rest of my life would make me happier. A wave of euphoria swept over my body as I came and came and came.

But then I noticed something was wrong. I couldn't stop ejaculating. My penis continued to gush large amounts of goo inside of her. The more I came, the thicker the spurts. The way Dokura casually stared at me, it was as if she knew this was going to happen. She had done something to me. I tried to pull myself out of her, but she pinned me down, holding me in place as I came into her.

"What's going on?" I asked, thrashing around in the nest.

"Why won't it stop?"

"Quit moving," she said. "I don't want to lose any of it."

The more I ejaculated, the weaker my muscles became. Dokura was able to hold me down effortlessly now. She kept me tightly inside her. She wanted to take in every drop of my semen.

I looked up at her powerful body as she stared down at me. I felt small and insignificant. By the time I finally finished coming, she removed my penis from inside of her and curled up around me.

"What the hell was that?" I asked, panting. "Why did I come like that?"

She stroked my hair.

"I'm sorry," she said. "I took a lot more out of you than I should have. But I needed the nutrients. We had been apart for so long."

As she pressed my face against her breasts, I began to calm down. I just laid on them like pillows, breathing furiously, exhausted. Her breasts seemed huge against my face. I didn't realize I had married a woman with breasts this big.

"I have no idea what you're talking about," I said, my words muffled in her cleavage.

"That's the way Usagi mate," she said.

"You say that as if Usagi aren't human."

"We're not human," she said.

I used all of my strength to lift my head to look at her. "Don't fuck around with me."

"We are hybrids," she said. "Centuries ago, an extraterrestrial ship crashed in the mountains between Europe and Asia. My alien ancestors mated with the humans in the area. After a few generations, the Usagi race was born."

Crawling out of bed, I wobbled to my feet.

"We spread throughout the world, mating with humans of all nationalities, increasing our numbers. These days we look far more human than alien. Only our eyes and ears remain."

I went for the tights I would have to use as pants.

"Where are you going?" she asked, staring at me as I searched the room.

"I'm through with this shit," I said. "You people are insane. I need to call my lawyer to get me out of this."

"You can't leave," she said. "You're an Usagi husband now. Your job is to stay in the nest during the mating period."

I found the tights under Dokura's wedding gown and pulled them on. They stretched all the way up to my nipples, then slid off my body onto the floor. The tights were too big. They didn't fit me anymore.

"How come these are so loose?" I said.

Then I looked around the room. I realized everything was a bit larger than it had been when we first arrived.

"What the fuck's going on?" I asked, realizing that the room had not gotten bigger. I had gotten smaller.

Dokura sat up and held her belly at me. Her stomach was fat all of a sudden, as if she were already five months pregnant.

"I told you," she said. "I needed the nutrients."

"I've shrunk by at least a foot!"

Not only was her stomach swollen, but her breasts were larger. Extra breasts were also beginning to swell beneath her ten additional nipples.

"Usagi mate differently from humans," she said. "When humans mate, the male gives the female his seed. Then the female extracts nutrients from her own body to form the baby inside of her. With Usagi, the female extracts the nutrients from the male's body to form her offspring."

"That's part of me inside of you?" I yelled, pointing at her swollen belly.

She nodded, casually. "I absorbed some of your mass to feed our babies."

"Babies? Plural?"

"Usagi produce litters of six to twelve offspring," she said. "Because it is so many, the male's nutrients are required during the entire gestation period."

"I don't believe this shit," I told her. "Am I going to be short for the rest of my life now? Am I going to grow back?"

She said, "My alien ancestors did have a regenerative power that allowed the males of their species to renew their lost mass after it had been absorbed by their mates. But when the aliens interbred with humans, it didn't work the same way. Humans don't have the same regenerative powers."

"I was a perfect six foot one before sleeping with you. Now I'll be lucky if I'm five foot one."

"You'll be getting a lot shorter than that during the gestation period," she said to me.

"What do you mean by that?"

"We must make love regularly in order to feed our babies the nutrients they need to grow big and strong," she said. "You want what's best for them, don't you?"

"Wait a minute..." I said. "Just how short am I supposed to get? How much of my nutrients do your babies need?"

Dokura stared at me for a few minutes. Then she blinked.

"All of it," she said.

I was taken aback.

"What do you mean all of it?" I asked.

"I mean all of you, your entire body, will be absorbed into my womb by the end of the gestation period," she said. "It's the way that Usagi mate."

"I don't get it," I said. I was pretty sure I understood what she meant, but I didn't want to believe it. "My entire body?"

"Every time we have sex, my body will absorb a little of your mass," she said. "You will become smaller and smaller over time, until you're all gone."

I stared into her eyes for a moment.

"I will just...die?"

"You will die so that our babies will live," she said.

"So you're saying that I should have chosen an eighteen year jail sentence over marrying you, correct? Because I'd much rather go to jail than die, thank you very much."

"But you're not going to jail. We've already been married."

"I think I'll call the cops on myself and have them bring

me in," I told her, putting my wedding suit and shoes back on. "I would definitely prefer that to allowing you to absorb me to death like the fucking blob."

I went for the door.

"You can't leave," she said. Her voice was calm and emotionless as usual, yet there was a slight hint of panic behind it.

"I don't want to die," I said.

"But what about the children?" she asked.

"Absorb somebody else," I told her, then stepped outside.

She ran after me, naked, into the snow.

"It can't be anyone else," she said. "It has to be you."

I jogged down the road, away from her.

"You don't understand what will happen..." she yelled after me.

I looked back at her but I didn't stop. She stood there in the snow, naked, her eyes glowing in the dark. Despite her nudity, the cold temperature didn't bother her. Although she looked human, at that moment I could finally tell that she was far from it.

CHAPTER FOURTEEN

My muscles were weak, my mind was fuzzy, and it was cold as hell, but I wasn't going to stop. I felt like the energy had been drained from every inch of my body, even my hair. My bones felt brittle. All I wanted to do was sleep. But I couldn't turn back.

I hiked all the way back to the highway within an hour. There were no cars on the road. I waited for a while, looking for a car I could wave down. Then I realized nobody was going to stop for a guy wearing see-through tights instead of pants in the middle of nowhere while it was snowing. So I followed the highway for about half an hour until I came to a rest area. It was the same rest stop I had been to before, where I met Dokura for the first time.

Just as it had been that night, the rest stop was empty. I wondered why they would bother putting a rest stop way out here if nobody ever stopped at it. Seemed like a waste of tax dollars. Part of me wondered if anybody would ever show up if I just waited there until morning.

There was a pay phone near the bathrooms. I didn't have any change on me, but I could at least dial emergency numbers. I dialed the one at the top of the list.

"I need help," I said, once I got a hold of an operator. "I'm stranded in this snowstorm and freezing to death. I'm at a rest area on Highway 9. I'm on foot. There's nobody for miles around."

I didn't want to tell her the whole truth. Mentioning what had really happened to me seemed like the wrong thing to say. They wouldn't take me seriously if I mentioned that I was forced to marry a half-alien woman who wanted to fuck me to death. All I really needed was a ride out of there, from anyone.

After I explained my dilemma to the operator, she seemed

perfectly willing to assist me, though she didn't treat it as all that big of an emergency. The big problem I had was trying to explain where I was exactly.

"What highway was that again?" she asked.

"It's a rest area off Highway 9," I said.

"I don't see a Highway 9," the woman said.

"It's not a major highway," I said. "Very few people seem to take this stretch of road."

It took the woman ten minutes just to figure out which highway I was on, and once she found it she couldn't figure out where on the highway I was. The road curled through the mountains and was over eighty miles long.

"I don't see any rest area on this road," the woman said.

"It's probably right in the middle. I've stopped here before." She still couldn't find it. She got her supervisor.

"Do you mean the Usagi rest area?" asked the supervisor.

"It's called the Usagi rest area?" I asked.

"The Usagi tribe pay for the rest stop," he said. "It's on their reservation. The majority of that stretch of highway is on their land."

"Just get me out of here."

"We'll send somebody to pick you up right away."

As I hung up the phone, I realized I couldn't feel my hands anymore. This wasn't necessarily a bad thing for my hand that had lost a finger but I knew I had to get warm. Inside the bathroom, it wasn't much warmer. A draft blew through the open space between the walls and ceiling. I tried doing jumping jacks to warm up, but was too weak for physical exertion. So I curled up in the corner of the handicapped bathroom stall and blew on my fingers and kneecaps.

While sitting there, I wondered why the emergency operators called the Usagi a tribe. Were they just mistaking the Usagi for a Native American tribe? Part of me wondered if the government already knew all about this hybrid race of aliens living amongst us, registered them as a tribe, put them on their own reservation, and let them do whatever they wanted to do.

The first thing I planned to do when I got out of there was to call my lawyer/swinger friend, Dave. That guy would be able to get me out of all of this. That son of a bitch fought dirty in the courtroom. He was the kind of lawyer you only wanted on your side, because he would tear you apart if you went up against him. If I had change for a phone call, I would have called him right away, even though it was the middle of the night.

Then I wondered if there was a way I could call him. I wondered if collect calls still existed. I wondered if I remembered how to even make a collect call anymore. Without wasting any more time, I went back out to the pay phone and realized I could pay for a call by entering in my credit card information. I guessed change didn't matter anymore as long as you had your credit card number memorized.

I was expecting to have to try him multiple times before he'd answer, but Dave picked up the phone on the first ring as if it were a normal time for him to be expecting calls. I told him about how I needed legal help. I told him about how I knocked up an Usagi girl.

"An Usagi?" he asked. "Are you kidding me?"

"You've heard of them?"

"I know all about them," he said. "And trust me, you do not want to marry an Usagi woman."

"Tell me about it."

"Listen to me very carefully," he said to me. "Whatever you do, don't go through with the ceremony. If the cops threaten to take you to jail, you let them. It will be much easier to get you out of this if you aren't legally bound."

"I already went through with the ceremony," I said, my voice quivering. "Dave, she bit my finger off."

"Shit..."

Then there was a silence on the other end.

"Did you sign the wedding papers?" he asked.

"Uh, no, I don't think so," I said.

"Are you sure?"

I thought about it for a second. "I definitely didn't sign any paperwork."

"Good, then the ceremony didn't mean shit. You're not actually married yet."

I sighed with relief.

"Worst case scenario you'll have to go to jail for a while," Dave said. "But at least you'll survive."

"You know about the Usagi mating habits?" I asked him.

"I had to defend one once," he said. "I learned a lot about them during that case and I have to say it was the kind of information I would have preferred to have stayed ignorant to. It was a time in my life I would have preferred to forget."

As we told each other everything we knew, a pair of headlights appeared in the distance, heading down the highway in this direction. It must have been my ride.

"Look," Dave said. "You've gotten yourself into some sensitive territory here. Trials involving the Usagi happen behind closed doors. Nobody wants to admit these people even exist."

The headlights came closer and slowed down as they approached the rest area.

"Your best option would be to stay as far away from them as possible. They won't hesitate to lock you in a basement somewhere until you're completely...digested. That's the way they used to do it in the old days. And they always got away with it. No body, no evidence."

"So what should I do now?" I asked him.

"We should meet up as soon as possible," he said. "Where are you now?"

"I'm actually at a rest stop," I said. "In Usagi territory."

There was a pause.

"What? You're at that rest stop?"

"Yeah, I just got away from them," I said. "The cops are coming to pick me up."

"That's the last place in the world you want to be," he said. "That's their fucking hunting ground. Forget the cops. Get the hell out of there. Now."

"The cops are already here," I said, as the car pulled into the rest area.

"You can't trust them," Dave said. "The cops in that area aren't going to help you."

When the cops saw me, their lights flashed on and their siren yelped. They zoomed up alongside the pay phone and the next thing I knew they had guns pointed at my head. They told me to drop the phone and raise my hands. I complied.

CHAPTER FIFTEEN

In the back of the cop car, soaking wet tights made me feel naked again. Just like last time. I could have sworn the two cops were the exact same cops that had picked me up that night. One had the same blond mustache and another had the same gray eyes. Only they didn't seem to recognize me.

They didn't speak to me as they got on the highway. Instead of going into town, they took the small country road back toward the Usagi village.

"You can't take me back there," I told them.

But they didn't stop.

"If you do as you're told we won't have to take you in," said Gray Eyes. "A Mrs. Silivasi reported that you were trying to escape your court-ordered wedding. All you need to do is sign the marriage documents and you'll be free to go."

"I'm not going to sign the papers," I said.

"It's either that or we take you in."

"Then take me in," I yelled.

But they didn't listen to me. They kept driving.

When we got back to the village, we drove up to a small group of Usagi women gathered near the church. They wore fluffy feathered robes over black lace nightgowns.

"Don't even think about running," said Blond Mustache, as he released me from the handcuffs and brought me to the Usagi.

Mrs. Silivasi, Dokura, her sisters, and a few older women were all there with their glowing stares and blank expressions. I couldn't look them in the eyes.

The matriarch handed the legal documents to the policemen.

"If he signs these we'll drop the charges," she said to them.

"What charges?" I asked.

"Running out on your family," she said.

As the papers were handed to me, I tossed them into the snow.

"I'm not signing these," I said to the cops. "Please, take me to jail."

"You're being incredibly difficult," said Gray Eyes, retrieving the papers from the snow. "Just sign the papers so we can go home."

"You don't understand," I said to them. "They want to kill me." I held up my hand. "Look, they cut my finger off."

The cops were surprised to see my bloodied hand and missing finger. Even though I whined and complained about it when they cuffed me, they still hadn't noticed it until now.

I showed them my brand. "They burned me, too."

The cops examined the burned vagina-shaped mark on my chest.

"They're a cult of psychopaths," I said. "You can't leave me with them."

I decided not to mention that they were also aliens.

Gray Eyes examined my hand. Then he looked at the Usagi women.

"Is this true, Mrs. Silivasi?" he asked. "Did you cut off his finger?"

Mrs. Silivasi shook her head. "He offered his finger to my daughter voluntarily. It was a part of our wedding ceremony. We didn't do anything to him against his will."

The cop looked back at me. "Is that how it happened?"

"I didn't have a choice," I said. "I thought I would have to go to jail if I didn't let her bite my finger off."

"But you did agree to it, correct?"

I looked at the cops, flustered, holding up my bloody hand. "But they bit my fucking finger off!"

"It sounds like you're the one responsible for your finger loss," said Gray Eyes. "Your charges won't stick. You might as well drop it."

"At least take me to the fucking hospital," I cried.

"Stop being such a wimp," said Blond Mustache.

"I'm missing a fucking finger here!"

"If you swear one more time you're getting a ticket," said Blond Mustache.

I wondered if he'd take me in if I punched him in the face.

Gray Eyes held out a pen and the documents.

"Just sign these," he said.

I shook my head.

"You've already said your vows in front of everyone," said Mrs. Silivasi.

"That's right," Gray Eyes said. "You're already married in front of God and the world. These papers are just a formality."

"I don't care."

"Be a man," Blond Mustache said. "Take responsibility for your actions like a grown-up."

"It's not that," I said. "They want to kill me."

"I'm losing patience here," said Gray Eyes.

"I won't sign it," I said. "Take me to jail. Now."

"You're not going to jail," he said, raising his voice.

I grabbed the papers, trying to rip them up. But the cop pulled them away, blocking me with his shoulder. I crumpled the edges, but couldn't rip into them.

Blond Mustache came at me from behind, as the contract slipped from my fingers.

"Arrest me," I cried.

Then I kicked Gray Eyes in the testicles and slapped him across the ear.

"Just take me to jail!"

The Usagi women stood there motionless, watching as Blond Mustache tackled me to the ground and put me back into the handcuffs. As I lay with my belly in the snow, I laughed. Maybe I had assaulted a police officer, but at least they were going to take me in. I waited for them to put me back into the cop car.

Then Gray Eyes kicked me in the stomach, while I was on the ground.

"Why would we take you to jail?" Gray Eyes said, kicking me in the stomach again. "You've done nothing wrong."

Blond Mustache kicked me from the other side.

"Yeah," said Blond Mustache, "we escorted you back to Mrs. Silivasi." He kicked me again. "And then you fully cooperated with us by signing the appropriate documents you were handed."

Gray Eyes kicked me in the face. "And then we left you with the beautiful mother of your child who you said you would never want to part from ever again."

When they were finished beating me in the snow, I looked up to see Mrs. Silivasi signing the contracts for me. She had my wallet out—the one that Dokura had stolen two months ago from the rest stop—copying my signature from the back of a credit card.

"I'll sign as a witness," said Blond Mustache, taking the pen from Mrs. Silivasi.

Both of the cops signed as witnesses.

As Gray Eyes dropped the contract back into his car, he said, "We'll make sure to deliver these documents personally, Mrs. Silivasi."

"Thank you very much," she replied to the officers.

"It's not my signature," I moaned from the ground. "You're committing fraud."

"It's over, kid," said Blond Mustache. "Let it go."

Then my face fell back into the snow.

The cops escorted me in handcuffs back to my wedding home. I was too tired to resist.

"I apologize for kicking you back there," I said to Gray Eyes. "I just wanted you to arrest me. If you leave me with them I'm going to die."

The cop was silent for a few feet.

Then he said, softly behind my ear as if he didn't want his partner to hear, "I know, kid. I'm sorry."

"You knew about this?"

He sighed loudly into my ear.

"It's out of my hands," he said. "There's nothing I can do."

"You could get me the hell out of here," I said.

My voice was loud enough to draw the others' attentions. Gray Eyes went silent and wouldn't speak to me again after that. After the cops tossed me into my wedding nest-bed and uncuffed me, they turned around and got the heck out of there as quickly as they could.

Dokura sat down in the nest next to me, placing her hands on my face, caressing the wounds the cops had given me. It was almost as if she felt sorry for what had happened.

From the doorway, Mrs. Silivasi said, "You will not escape your fatherly duties. I will make sure of that."

After she closed the door, I heard a jangling key enter the door's knob. Then she locked it from the outside. When I looked around the room, I realized all of the walls, doors, and windows were reinforced. The place was designed to keep people in. This wasn't just my new family home. It was also a prison.

CHAPTER SIXTEEN

I was too tired and in too much pain to move. Dokura quietly removed my wet clothes, and then removed her clothes. She pulled the blankets over us and wrapped herself around me, hugging me tightly to her chest. The way she held me seemed both comforting and constricting, like she was expressing her love at the same time as holding me in place so that I wouldn't try to escape ever again.

I thought about what Dave said. The Usagi could just lock me away with my wife until I was completely absorbed and nobody would hear from me again. But I knew there was still hope. Dave knew what had happened to me. He knew I was captured by the cops at the rest area on Highway 9. He'd know exactly where they took me and would get help. It was only a matter of time before he got me out of this mess. I couldn't just let them kill me. My life was too important. I was the best damned editor in the publishing industry. My authors needed me. If it weren't for my expertise my writers never would have gone as far as they did. I had a responsibility to them. I had to keep their dreams alive. For their sake, I had to survive.

"I don't want to die," I said out loud.

Dokura thought I was talking to her. She hushed me and then caressed my hair on the side of my face, petting me like a cat.

"I know," she said. "It's difficult becoming a father."

As I drifted off to sleep, I felt the bulge of her belly pressed against my back. Movement came from within, churning and shifting. At first, I thought it was her children making the movements, but then I realized it was the part of me that she had absorbed. It emitted a low gurgling sound as her body digested it, converting me into food for the babies growing inside of her.

When I awoke the next morning, we were in the same position. It seemed as if she had been awake the whole time, just holding me and staring at the back of my head.

"Good morning," she said to me, as she realized I was awake.

Then she rubbed her hand down my chest toward my penis. Before she could grab onto it, I pushed her hand away.

"No," I told her.

"It's time for another feeding," she said, rubbing my inner thigh and breathing against my neck.

"Didn't you get enough last night?" I asked.

"We have a lot of catching up to do," she said. "My womb has been starving these past two months."

She wrapped one arm around my neck, putting me in a headlock with one hand as she grabbed my penis with her other.

"Besides," she said, "Mother told me that I need to make you smaller." She held me in place. I could feel my penis getting hard in her hand. "So that you will be more manageable."

I was only a few inches shorter than she was, so I wasn't so small yet that she could overpower me. But I felt as if all my energy had been drained. I was too sore to move. So I came up with another strategy. Instead of resisting her, I got into it more, trying to ejaculate while she was jerking me off. If I had a regular orgasm I wouldn't be able to get it up again for hours.

When she noticed I was becoming more compliant, she sucked on my ear.

"That's it," she said. "Enjoy it. Most Usagi males get excited by the idea of being absorbed by their females."

I could already feel an orgasm coming on. When Dokura released my penis, I grabbed it and continued jerking off. She didn't see me doing it beneath the covers as she climbed on top of me. I ejaculated just before she could mount me.

She paused when she felt my cum hit her thigh, staring at me blankly. Then she pulled the cover off to see the semen covering the bed. But it didn't seem to bother her.

"We can't be wasteful," she said.

With her index finger, she swabbed up the glob of cum on her thigh, then brought it toward her crotch and pushed it up inside of her.

"Every single drop is important," she said.

Her vagina sucked on her fingers as if it were a mouth sucking on a lollipop. My eyes widened when I saw it happen. She had total control of her vaginal muscles. When the glob was all the way inside, the vagina closed its lips and swallowed.

Then she squatted down on the bed toward the puddle of semen. Her labia opened wide and slurped up the goop. It looked like a snail feeding on algae as her vagina slid up the bed, ingesting every droplet. When it was all absorbed, Dokura lowered her vagina onto my thigh. It felt exactly like a mouth sucking on my leg as she drank every drop of sperm. After it was all cleaned up, her vaginal lips sucked on the head of my penis, slurping up a bead of cum that was oozing out of the hole. Then she sucked the rest of my flaccid penis inside of her, to make sure she didn't miss any.

Before I realized what was happening, my penis was becoming erect. Even though I just had an orgasm, the sensation of her vagina sucking on me was too big of a turn on to resist.

"That's it," she said. "Give me more."

Her vagina gave me a blowjob. The best I'd ever had. I think something cracked inside me at that moment. Even though I knew what was going to happen, I didn't want it to stop. Maybe it's human nature. Maybe it's because I'm a guy. Or maybe it's because Dokura's vaginal juices contained a chemical that acted as an aphrodisiac. Whatever it was, I suddenly found myself believing that having sex with Dokura right at that moment was the most important thing I could be doing in the world. I didn't care about the consequences. I just wanted to be inside her.

As she fucked me, Dokura wouldn't stop staring me in the eyes. She panted furiously, crying out in ecstasy. It was the most emotion I had ever seen her exhibit. When she stared into my eyes, it was like she was reading my mind. It was as if she could see my desire to be inside of her, and that turned her on even more.

"I want you inside of me," she cried, thrusting her pelvis against me, her labia tugging madly on my cock. "I want all of you inside of me."

Just before I came, I could feel every particle of my body being pulled toward her crotch. It was as if her vagina had its own gravity—a black hole that wanted to pull me within. When I exploded inside of her, she squealed in an insect-like way that startled me. The ejaculation was thicker and more powerful than it was the last night. But this time I was more sober. I felt myself shrinking as I came. I felt the cells in my body liquefying and exiting my body like sperm.

As my orgasm continued, I recognized a new sensation. It didn't feel as if my penis were ejaculating the fluids into her. It felt more like her pussy was sucking the fluids out of me. My insides were liquefying and she was drinking them from my penis like a milkshake through a straw. A part of me was horrified by this realization, but another part of me liked it. The orgasm kept going and I didn't want it to ever stop.

Unfortunately, while looking in Dokura's eyes I could tell that she too didn't want it to ever stop. So she kept going. She kept sucking the nutrients out of me. I felt myself getting smaller by the minute.

"Dokura..." I said.

She immediately knew, just by looking at me, that I thought she was going too far. But her appetite was insatiable. She wanted to take in as much of me as she could. Her eyes closed shut and she ravenously fed on me, absorbing me.

After a few more minutes, it no longer felt as if I were shrinking. It felt more like Dokura was growing. Her body became heavy. All twelve of her breasts expanded—the extra ones filled out to the size of natural breasts. Her entire abdomen swelled, covering half of my body. It didn't feel like a pregnant belly. It felt like a water balloon made of human skin, filled with warm water.

When she was finished, she fell onto the bed next to me, exhausted, breathing heavily. She was so bloated she could hardly move. It seemed like the reason she stopped was not because she wanted to, but because she didn't have the energy to go on.

I looked at my hands and my feet, then compared myself to Dokura. She had taken in about fifty pounds of my body. I was now the size I was when I was eleven years old. Even if I got out of this mess, I was doomed to have the body of a child for the rest of my life.

"Sorry for pigging out on you," Dokura said, rubbing my arm and catching her breath. "My mother always used to say I was the gluttonous one."

I rolled against her garbage bag-sized stomach and looked up at her. My energy level was so low I could hardly keep my eyes open.

"Thank you," Dokura said, and then kissed me on the forehead "This should keep our babies fed for a long time."

Then she closed her eyes and cradled her massive belly. A satisfied look stretched across her face. As I lay weakened and shriveled next to her, I was suddenly filled with resentment. I felt as if I had been used and manipulated. I had no idea what had come over me or why I wanted her to absorb me like that. I promised myself that I wouldn't let it happen again. My survival depended on it.

CHAPTER SEVENTEEN

Dokura spent the day curled up around her belly. She didn't pay much attention to me anymore. She didn't need to. She had gotten what she wanted from me. Now I had lost my appeal. Her focus was mostly on her stomach. She stared at it, as if imagining what her children looked like inside of her. Neither of us left the bed for anything, except to use the bathroom.

"I'm surprised you're hanging around in here all day," I said to her. "I'm the one who's imprisoned. Aren't you free to go whenever you want?"

Dokura lay beside me, caressing a row of six breasts. "Both the male and female Usagi stay in the nest during the entire gestation period."

"Even if I wasn't trying to escape I would have had to stay here?" I asked.

She nodded.

"We just lie together and keep warm," she said. "When the babies require nutrients, we make love. We never leave the nest."

"Does your family at least come to visit you?"

She shook her head. "Nobody's allowed to disturb the nest. Not until the children are able to walk on their own."

"What about food?" I said. "How are we supposed to eat?"

Her eyes bored into me.

"You're the food," she said.

Then she caressed my cheek.

"What do you mean?"

"Your body provides nourishment for our whole family." She rubbed her swollen belly. "As I absorb you, my body also feeds on your nutrients as they feed the children."

"How does that feed me?"

She grabbed one of her breasts. "Once my body processes your nutrients, my breasts will begin to produce milk. It is what will nourish our children after they are born. But before they are born, it is what will nourish you."

"I'm supposed to be breastfed by my wife?" I asked.

She nodded her head. "It will sustain you."

I looked at her breasts, wondering what it would be like to drink from them. Then I shook my head at the thought.

"We will never have to leave our nest for the entire gestation period," she said. "You're all the food we'll need."

"So I'm basically just a packed lunch that you get to fuck?" I said. Then I chuckled, even though there wasn't anything funny about it.

She patted my head and looked me in the eyes.

"Exactly," she said.

"I was joking."

I should have known not to joke with an Usagi. I doubted they even knew what jokes were.

"You were correct," she said. "The father's role is basically as you said—to be a packed lunch."

"Why would any man ever agree to that?" I asked her. "Even Usagi males couldn't possibly want to volunteer for such a role."

"Of course they do," Dokura said. "It is the way Usagi bear their young. It is the most beautiful thing in the world."

CHAPTER EIGHTEEN

The next day, two police cars pulled into the Usagi village. I peeked through one of the small circular windows, wondering what was going on. When I saw Dave step out of one of the cars, with two officers from the city by his side, I exhaled with relief.

"Dave, you beautiful son of a bitch," I said.

Dokura looked up from the bed.

"What's going on?" she asked me.

"A friend of mine has come," I said. "He's getting me out of here."

She stared at me blankly.

"You're not going anywhere," she said. "You have to be a father."

"I don't have to be anything I don't want to be."

Outside, Dave was waving papers in Mrs. Silivasi's face. She shook her head at him. He began to shout and point at the cop cars. Whatever he said, she appeared to become more compliant. A few minutes later, they came to our house.

"Open this up," I heard Dave say, as keys rattled by the door handle.

Dokura didn't move from the bed, staring up with little interest.

"Nobody can disturb their nest," Mrs. Silivasi said to the lawyer.

"I'm not going to disturb it," he said. "He's going to come out to me."

When the door opened, I saw Dave standing there with his cutthroat lawyer-face on. He was like a capitalistic angel with a blue striped tie.

"You came," I said, wrapping a blanket around my waist.

He tossed me some clothes. "Put these on. Spandex. One size fits most."

I put on the spandex pants and shirt.

"I'm legally not allowed to enter," he said. "But you can come out."

"Am I free to go?" I asked.

84

"We're not out of the water yet," he said. "Come outside and we'll talk about it."

I looked back at Dokura as I went toward the door. Her expression was unchanged.

Outside, one of the policemen put an electronic cuff around my leg. The cop had a blond mustache and looked exactly like the previous cop I had seen, but this one was wearing a different uniform. It couldn't have been the same guy.

"You're not legally allowed to keep him locked in this house anymore," Dave told Mrs. Silivasi. "He's only under house arrest for the time being."

"What does that mean?" I asked, as the cop flicked the mechanism on.

"You're not allowed to leave Usagi territory," he said. "You can go as far as the rest area to make phone calls. If you attempt to leave the perimeter, the authorities will be alerted. Same thing will happen if you tamper with the device."

"I'm still going to be stuck here?" I asked.

"Just until after the trial," he said.

"When's the trial?" I asked.

Dave looked over at Mrs. Silivasi and the cops.

"I need some time alone with my client," he said to them, then turned to my mother-in-law. "Anywhere private we can meet?"

"Only the woods are private here," she said.

"Fine," he said.

He led me away from the village into the woods. Pine needles stabbed into my bare feet as I walked, but the hope Dave was bringing me lessened the pain.

As we walked, he slapped me on the back.

"What the heck happened to you, shorty?" he asked. Then he chuckled. "You look like my nephew. Couldn't you have kept it in your pants for one day?"

"I tried."

"You also went ahead and signed the papers when I told you not to."

"I didn't sign them. The cops beat the crap out of me and forged my signature."

He nodded. "Sounds about right. But never mind about that. It wouldn't have mattered anyway."

He sat me down on a tree stump and gave me a serious look.

"What's the matter?" I asked him.

He looked off into the distance and scratched his nose, trying to find the right words. I didn't know if I wanted to hear what he was about to say.

Then he turned to me and said, "This whole mess is a lot more complicated than I was hoping for."

"Complicated how?"

"The new government, the new court system—they're going to cause us problems. After discussing your case with the board, it seems like they might side with the Usagi on this."

"What do you mean?" I asked. "The Usagi want to kill me. Murder is illegal. I'm in the right. End of story."

"It's not as simple as that," he said. "You see, your DNA has been bonded to the children growing inside of that Usagi wife of yours. Only you can father them."

"So what?"

He sighed and shook his head.

"If they let you go and your wife is no longer able to feed on you, the babies are going to die. They'll be stillborn."

"So what?"

"So it would be considered abortion," he said. "Abortion is a bigger crime than murder these days. And in your case, if you run out on your wife, you will cause up to twelve abortions at once, depending on the size of her litter. They won't allow that to happen."

I choked on my words as I tried to speak. "But the babies aren't even fucking born yet. I'm alive! Are they going to just let the Usagi kill me?"

"The courts won't see it that way. They'll see it as saving the lives of twelve babies."

"But that's like forcing a healthy living human to be an organ donor," I said. "All the organs could save a dozen people at the cost of only one man's life, but that doesn't justify murder."

He shook his head at me. "That's a good argument, but they won't see it as the same thing. The difference is you chose to have sex with the woman in the first place. You're the reason she's pregnant. Now they think you have to be responsible for those children, no matter what the cost. They think you should freely give up your life and allow your wife to assimilate you so that your children will survive."

"Assimilate me?" I asked.

"That's what they're calling it," he said. "They don't say you're being devoured. They say you're just being assimilated. It makes them feel as if they aren't exactly sentencing you to death."

"But what about my rights?" I asked. "I don't have the right to survive?"

"We live in a fucked up world these days," he said. "If a pregnant mother has cancer and the only way to save her life is to go through chemo, she's not allowed to do it anymore because it could harm the fetus inside of her. Whenever a choice has to be made to save either the mother or the unborn child, the child will always be saved. The mother won't have a say in the matter. It's the same situation you're in now. There is a choice between saving your life and saving the lives of the children. They will not likely side with you."

"So how the hell am I going to get out of this?" I asked.

"Well, it's not hopeless yet, not by a long shot. Nothing like this has happened before. It will really challenge our government's current ideologies. Plus, what they really want is for this to go away as soon as possible. We can use that to our advantage. What they want is an alternative solution, so they don't have to make the decision. They're hoping you'll just agree to be assimilated like a good little boy. But that's not the only alternative."

"What else can be done?"

"We need to figure out a way to keep the babies alive without you having to sacrifice yourself for them."

"Is that possible?"

"That's what we're banking on," he said. "These Usagi have been living primitive lives for centuries. They haven't even tried to find an alternative solution. I'm sure there are doctors out there who can figure out a reasonably simple way to keep both you and the children alive. Maybe a dietary supplement that can be bio-engineered from your DNA. Maybe they can move each of the fetuses into the wombs of twelve human women. There's got to be another way. This won't just be good for you, it will be good for all the Usagi people. They might not have to be hidden away from the rest of society like monsters anymore."

"You really think it could work?" I asked.

"I know it could," he said. Then he paused for a moment. "That is, if we have the money..."

"Don't worry about the money," I said. "I'll pay whatever it takes. You know that won't be a problem."

"It's not just the money. It also depends on time."

"How much time do we have?" I asked.

"Only a month to find an alternative solution," he said. "That's when the trial will take place. If I can offer up a way to keep you alive without aborting the babies you'll be good to go. You'll still have to stay married to the woman and raise all of the kids with her, but at least you will survive."

"What if you don't find another solution?" I asked.

"It will be...a lot more difficult to save you," he said. "But still not impossible. Let's just hope it doesn't come to that."

"So what am I supposed to do for the next month?" I asked.

"Practice something I normally would never ask anyone to practice... abstinence." Then he chuckled at himself. "You're not yet legally obligated to feed yourself to your wife. She's probably been fed plenty of you already. If we lose the battle, the feeding will resume, but for now you're okay."

He helped me to my feet.

"Just resist the temptation to fuck her," he said. "It's going to be hard for you, though. Mating with an Usagi will change your natural instincts. Your brain is being reprogrammed as we speak. Within a few weeks you'll probably be begging your wife to assimilate you. You have to have willpower. And I mean Buddhist monk willpower."

"I'll work on that," I said.

"And whatever you do, don't drink your wife's breast milk," he said. "That stuff will really mess you up. It's full of endorphins, aphrodisiacs, and all kinds of chemicals you do not want to be ingesting. It will make you totally compliant to anything she wants you to do. It's how the Usagi women get their males to submit to being devoured alive."

"I'll keep that in mind," I said.

"I'll have a guy bring real food out to you once a week until the trial," he said. "Also, I notified your mother about your situation. She has visitation rights. She said she'll be flying in from Phoenix next week to check up on you."

"Thanks," I told him, "but you really didn't have to do that."

The last thing I wanted to do was bring my mom into all of this. The woman was a walking nightmare.

"Outside of drinking the breast milk and having sex, I want you to do pretty much anything the Usagi tell you. Don't try to escape. Don't cause any trouble. Be nice. It will be a lot easier for us that way."

"What if they want to bite off more of my fingers?" I asked, holding up my four-fingered hand.

Dave shrugged. "I guess you'll just have to politely decline. If that doesn't work then give me a call and I'll sort it out for you."

I nodded, staring at the space where my finger used to be.

"Well, I think that about covers everything," he said, patting me on the back. "You've sure gotten yourself into quite a mess, but nothing old Davy Boy can't fix for you."

As he stood in front of me, I found myself bowing at him. I didn't know how else to thank him. I just bowed at him as a sign of appreciation for all he was doing for me.

"My life is in your hands," I said. "Please don't let them kill me."

He just smiled in response and patted me on the shoulder again.

I had a warm hopeful feeling as I walked Dave back to the cop cars. But as I watched him drive away, into the forest, that warm feeling mutated into a feeling of dread. I realized that my lawyer friend hadn't actually done much to resolve my situation. There were a lot of promises, but not much else. In fact, the tracking mechanism on my leg made it even more difficult for me to escape. Sure, I was no longer forced to be locked in my house with my alien wife, but where else was I going to go? There wasn't a hotel in the area I could stay at. I was still in the exact same predicament I was in before he arrived.

As I walked back toward my wedding home, toward my nest, I realized that Dave had given me one thing. He had given me something to hold out for. He proved to me that I still had a chance.

When I entered my house and closed the door behind me to keep the cold air out, Dokura was still lying in the nest, staring at me.

"I told you that you're not going anywhere," she said. "You have to be a father."

I ignored her comment and sat on the floor with my back to her.

CHAPTER NINETEEN

For the next week, I didn't leave the nest much. My spandex clothes weren't warm enough to venture outside for too long. I only went down to the rest area to call my boss, but he told me that Dave had already gotten me time off for the month.

Luckily, Dokura hadn't been trying to have sex with me anymore. Still sated from the last time, she said she wouldn't have to feed again until her cravings came back. I was safe for the time being. However, she did continuously try to get me to drink her breast milk.

"You need to eat," she said, aiming her rack of breasts at me.

"I'm not hungry," I said.

"Of course you are," she said. "You haven't eaten in days."

"I'm fine," I said.

"I can hear your stomach growling," she said. "Come to me."

"No, thank you. I don't want any."

She poked at her swollen tits.

"They feel like they're ready to burst," she said. "Drink some before they begin to leak. I don't want to waste any."

"Drink it yourself, then," I said, dismissing her.

This was the same conversation I had been having with her all week. If she pushed it, I would leave the house for a while. I waited for the food delivery Dave said that he would send out. But nobody came. I didn't know how much longer I could hold out.

I spent a lot of my time staring out the windows at the Usagi going about their day-to-day business. A lot of them liked to wander around for no particular reason. None of them ever seemed in a hurry to get anywhere. I had no idea what they did for food or money.

The older man, Uncle Stefan, wandered between the houses one day. His strange, massive shadow dragged behind him. I still wondered what Mrs. Silivasi meant by his shadow being overweight. The idea was absurd.

"Why is Stefan's shadow like that?" I asked Dokura.

She seemed reluctant to respond at first, but then she said, "He's ashamed of it."

"How can a shadow be overweight?"

"It's the size he used to be, before mating."

"He survived mating?"

"Yes," she said. "He's the only Usagi male in our community who was unsuccessful at coupling. His wife died during their gestation period. All of the babies were lost. But he continued on. He is the saddest Usagi in the village."

"But what about his shadow?"

"When Usagi men are absorbed, their entire bodies shrink but their shadows remain the original size."

"That doesn't make any sense," I said.

But then I looked over at my own shadow and realized that it was too big for my eleven-year-old body, just as Uncle Stefan's shadow was too big for his scrawny frame.

"How is that possible?" I asked.

"It is your body playing tricks on you," she said. "In the old times, Usagi did not have mirrors. Shadows were the closest thing. While mating, if an Usagi husband's shadow stayed the same size he wouldn't realize he was shrinking."

"Physics and logic aside, why would his own body deceive him like that?"

"It's what happens to Usagi men. Your body will do whatever it takes to keep you feeding your mate, even if it has to trick your mind in order to do so."

When I looked out the window at the sad old man, I began to hope that I would be as lucky as he was. If Dokura happened to die during the gestation period I wouldn't have anything to worry about but the size of my shadow.

CHAPTER TWENTY

It was the day my mother was supposed to arrive and I was dreading it. I loved my mother, but she was a complete psychopath. Everyone says their mothers are psychopaths, but mine was about as crazy as one could get without being locked away from the rest of society.

For starters, let me give you an example: my mom was a reverse-kleptomaniac. At least that's what I always called it. A regular klepto might have a compulsion to sneak things out of stores, but my mother had a compulsion to sneak things into stores. You see, my mother loved cooking. She considered herself a professional chef, even though she had never had an actual cooking job in her whole life. Every time we went out to eat she raved about how she could have cooked the meal so much better and how it would have been so much cheaper. She said the same thing about anything sold in stores, apart from the raw ingredients.

She was so into cooking that she tried to start her own business. She created her own company called, "Emma's Home Cookin'," which made sauces, jellies, soups, frozen dinners, and other assorted food products. She even made little labels for her products with a hand-drawn logo on them. But she didn't know the first thing about running a business. She didn't have distributors. She tried selling her products to her friends, but they weren't buying them. So she started sneaking her food into grocery stores. She put them on the shelves or made little displays, peeled price tags off other products and stuck them to hers, then left them there hoping that customers of that store would buy and enjoy her products. She lost a lot of money doing this, but she didn't care. She just wanted people to have her products.

The stores caught on over time. She was arrested on more

than one occasion for this little scheme of hers. But she couldn't stop herself from doing it. For years, it was her obsession. The only reason she stopped was because she couldn't afford it anymore.

As a kid, there was nothing more embarrassing for me than the times my mother dragged me into the store to help her shelve her own products without getting caught. But she had a knack for embarrassing me no matter what I did with her. If she had a talent at all, she was talented at embarrassing people. She wasn't a talented cook, that's for sure.

When her car pulled into the Usagi village, I had to take some deep calming breaths. I could already hear her loud, manic voice, and she hadn't even turned the car's engine off yet.

"Oh, my!" she cried in the distance, to no one in particular. "Look at all these wonderful houses!"

I looked out the window, but couldn't see her yet. Many Usagi came out to greet her, including Mrs. Silivasi. When my mother met my mother-in-law, I heard loud excited yells echoing through the forest.

The only lines I could understand were: "Give me a hug!" and "We're family now!"

My mother was pretty much the exact opposite of an Usagi. She wore all of her emotion on her sleeve, at all times. Dave must not have explained the situation properly. Or maybe he did and she just wasn't listening. Or maybe he wasn't legally allowed to give her too much information about the Usagi. Whatever the reason, it sounded like she was here to celebrate my recent wedding, not comfort me in my hour of need.

"Where's my new daughter-in-law!" I heard my mom's giddy cry, running toward my wedding house. "Who's the beautiful woman who's finally making me a grandma!"

I sensed doom coming. I didn't want to have to explain the whole situation to my mother. She was all excited about having grandchildren and a new daughter-in-law. It was going to break her heart once she learned that this woman was actually an alien creature trying to kill me.

"You're not allowed to enter the nest during the gestation period," I heard Mrs. Silivasi tell my mother.

But, as always with her, the words just flew in one ear and out the other.

My mother opened the door.

"You're not allowed to see them," said Mrs. Silivasi.

My mom's flowery blue dress fluttered through the crack in the door as she waved away the Usagi matriarch and said, "Oh, nonsense! We're family now."

When she entered the house, she raised her arms wide and cried, "Hi sweetie!"

Then wrapped her arms around me so tight I felt as if my neck would break.

"I have a hair appointment at two so I can't stay long," my mother said, rubbing my shoulder. "I don't want to get in the way of you two honeymooners anyway."

She didn't seem to notice my height difference whatsoever.

When she saw Dokura sitting on the bed, she raised her arms into the air and squealed.

"You must be Dokura!" she cried, and ran to her.

She gave Dokura a big hug, but the Usagi only slightly hugged her back.

"Oh, you have the prettiest eyes!" she said. "I just love you!"

"Calm down, Mom," I told her.

"I can't help it," she said. "I'm so excited to have a new daughter in my life!"

My mother put her hand under the covers and felt Dokura's stomach.

"Oh, and she's so preggers!" her eyes lighting up as she touched my wife's belly.

Little did she know that her stomach wasn't swollen because she was pregnant, but because she had absorbed a quarter of my body last week.

"Oh, and she's got so many boobs!" my mom cried, counting each one. "Twelve of them!" Then she turned to me, "She's just like those girls you used to fantasize about as a teenager, eh moochy? I bet you feel lucky!"

I paused for a moment. Because she was not fazed by the fact that my wife had twelve breasts, I began to wonder if she knew more about the Usagi than I had assumed.

"I'm Emma, by the way," my mom said to Dokura, then she pointed at me, "that short guy's mom. And your mom now, too."

"Mom?" I said.

"How many babies are in an Usagi litter again?" she asked Dokura.

"Mom?"

"Up to twelve," Dokura said.

"Mom?"

"Twelve!" my mom cried. "I'm going to have twelve grand-babies! Oh my god, I can't wait!"

"Mom?"

After she finished jumping up and down, my mother finally realized I was trying to get her attention.

"You already know about what's happening here?" I asked her.

She waved me off. "Oh, yeah, your friend Dave told me everything. You really should have called me yourself though."

"So..." I began. "You know what's supposed to happen to me? You know I'm supposed to die?"

She suddenly put on a sad face and drooped over to me. "Oohhh, I know...I'm so sorry, moochy." She kissed my forehead. "But you're an Usagi now and that's a natural part of the Usagi lifecycle. We'll just have to cherish the time you have left."

After she pinched my cheek, she turned back to Dokura and her happy face returned.

"Not to mention you'll produce twelve grandchildren," she said to me while rubbing Dokura's belly. "How many men get to leave a legacy like that!"

"Wait a minute," I said, raising my voice. "You're okay with all of this?"

She looked back and groaned. "Well, of course I'm going to miss you...but you have to make the sacrifice for the sake of the children."

"I can't believe you're taking their side," I said. "They plan to end my life and you couldn't be happier."

She rolled her eyes. "Oh, don't be so melodramatic. They won't exactly end your life. More like...recycle it. It's very green!"

"What the hell are you talking about? They want to fucking kill me!"

"Language!" my mother cried. She never could handle the F-word.

After she shook off my outburst, she said, "You have to make sacrifices for your family. That's what it means to become a parent."

"That's easy for you to say. You didn't have to die in order to have kids."

My mom's tone became annoyed, as if I were being completely unreasonable.

"Don't you think you're being a little selfish?" she asked. "How do you think Dokura feels?" She rubbed my wife's shoulder. "After you're gone, she'll have to raise all twelve children all by herself. Now that's sacrifice. All you have to do is lie around and have sex for nine months."

"But I'll die!"

"We all die eventually," she said. "At least you'll die for a good cause."

I smacked my face and fought the urge to rip my brain out of my head. I was surprised I didn't predict this was how my mother would react to this situation. If she already had the power to transform me into twelve babies she would have done so years ago, just before I went off to college.

My mother looked back at my wife and smiled, brushing her hair out of her eyes.

"You're going to have such beautiful children," she said. "And if you ever need a babysitter just call Nana Emma. Any excuse to see the little angels and I'll be there."

As my mother pressed on Dokura's stomach, breast milk squirted out a few of the nearby nipples.

"Whoa there, momma!" she said, and giggled. "You're spraying."

"That's not supposed to happen," Dokura said.

"It's not?" My mother's mouth widened with concern. "What's wrong, darling?"

"My body's producing it for him," she said, pointing at me. "But he refuses to drink it."

"What?" My mother glared at me. "Why aren't you letting your wife breastfeed you?"

"Why?" I yelled. "Why do you think?"

"But you have to," she said, acting like an Usagi biology expert all of a sudden. "It's an important part of the pregnancy cycle. You're going to mess it up. If you make my grandkids sickly you're going to be in so much trouble!"

"I don't care. I'm not doing it."

"Typical." She shook her head and looked at Dokura. "Even as a baby he refused to nurse. I always had to force my boob into his mouth every single time." She looked over at me. "Is that what we're going to have to do? Force her boob into your mouth?" Then she looked back at Dokura. "Just hold his head in place and squirt a little in there. That always did the trick. Once it was on his tongue he would start sucking it up until my nipples felt like they were going to come off."

"Jesus Christ, Mom."

"Well, it worked when you were a baby, didn't it?"

I looked at Dokura. She was just sitting there calmly with no expression, yet it seemed like deep down she was getting a good kick out of my mom taking her side.

"It doesn't matter, anyway," I said. "Dave is working on an alternate solution to this problem. He's trying to find a method to bring the babies to term that won't result in my body being absorbed into Dokura's womb."

"How does he plan to do that?" my mother asked.

Dokura also seemed interested in what I had to say.

"I don't know yet," I said. "It sounded as if he wanted to figure out a way to feed Dokura some artificial bio-engineered flesh that could replace my own."

My mother's eyes widened. She stood up with panic across her face.

"Oh, no, no, no, no, no, no," she said. "You can't do that. That bio-engineered garbage will be full of horrible chemicals that will be harmful to your babies." She looked at my wife. "Dokura, don't listen to him. You have to eat him all up. That's all natural. It's the proper Usagi way."

"You don't know that it's harmful," I said. "It hasn't even been invented yet."

"No," she said to me. "It's final. You're going to do this the natural way. It's not worth risking the health of the children."

"My survival isn't worth the risk?"

"Don't let him weasel his way out of this," she said to my wife. "I want you to gobble him up whether he likes it or not."

Dokura nodded her head at my mother.

I said, "You're such a nightmare."

"Oh, don't worry about him," my mom told her. "He'll lighten up once he shrinks to a third his original size and realizes he's got nowhere else to go but up your honey pot."

Dokura nodded her head at my mother again.

I said, "How do you manage to say the exact worst thing you could possibly say at every available opportunity?"

But at this point my mother was just ignoring everything I had to say.

"I have to go now, sweetie," she said, hugging Dokura with all her strength. "I hope to see a lot more of you from now on. I'll need somebody in my life now that my scaredy-cat son won't be around for much longer."

When my mom came to me, I just shook my head at her.

"Come on, give me a hug, grouchy," she said. "You know I'm just joking."

She hugged me, but I didn't hug her back.

"I love you, moochy," she said.

"Yeah, sure you do." I dodged a kiss before she could plant one on my nose.

"Now be a good boy and fatten up your wife," she said as she went for the door. "I want my grandchildren to grow up to be big and strong."

When she left, I turned to my Usagi wife. Her blue eyes glowed at me.

"I like her," Dokura said.

But at the moment, I didn't share her sentiment one little bit.

CHAPTER TWENTY-ONE

Another week passed. Nobody ever arrived with food for me. I hadn't eaten for half of a month. If I weren't so weak and delirious I would have hiked down to the rest area and called Dave about it. He might have forgotten he made that promise or maybe Mrs. Silivasi was turning the delivery drivers away. Either way, one phone call would have straightened it all out. But there was no way I was able to make the hike anymore.

Dokura continued to try to get me to drink from her breasts with no success. She even tried to force her boob into my mouth as my mother suggested, but I bit onto her nipple until she pulled away. She didn't try that again. So she decided to wait for me to give in.

"You'll have to eat some time," she said. "You might as well stop torturing yourself."

More days passed. I wouldn't give in. The only thing I had energy to do, it seemed, was lie in bed and think and sleep, so that's what I did.

One night, I awoke to the taste of sweet caramel butter on my tongue. When I opened my eyes, I saw Dokura above me, squeezing droplets of her milk into my sleeping mouth. I was so weak, so hungry, that I didn't spit it back out. Her glowing eyes watched me as she dribbled more into my lips. My brain told me to close my mouth, but the rest of me wanted to keep it open.

She lowered herself onto my face and slipped one of her nipples between my lips. I just let it slide against my tongue for a while. I didn't want to suckle from it. If I was too weak to resist I was also too weak to give in. But then she squirted a gush of breast milk down my throat. It was warm and sweet, strangely hydrating yet also slightly salty.

Before I knew it, I was sucking furiously on her nipple, guzzling the fluids like a ravenous mutant man-baby. She pulled it out of my mouth and shoved another one between my lips, so I drank from that one for a while. Then she pulled that breast out and gave me some from another breast. She switched between them quickly, almost excitedly, as if she wanted to make sure I got to drink from each and every one of her twelve breasts.

When I was done, I physically felt wonderful, almost euphoric. But mentally I felt guilty and weak. I felt like a quitter. I knew that it would be more difficult to resist Dokura from that point on. My own emotions were working against me. My logic had to overpower those feelings.

Though only an hour later, I found myself crawling across the bed and into Dokura's arms. She wrapped me up in the blankets and pressed all twelve of her breasts against me. I fell asleep inside of her warmth, sucking on her nipples, drinking her intoxicating fluids in my dreams.

After a couple days of nursing, my strength returned. I felt twice as strong as ever. However, I didn't leave the bed at all. The bed had become so much cozier. I just felt like sleeping and snuggling against Dokura's warm body all day. I knew it was the effect of drinking the breast milk, but it felt so good I didn't care. The month was almost over anyway. It wouldn't be long before Dave got me out of this.

One strange effect the milk had on me was that it made me fall in love with Dokura. I was not just sexually attracted to her, I was infatuated with her. I lay in bed and told her how much I loved her all day long. She wrapped her arms around me and told me how much she loved me. But I knew it was bullshit. I knew I didn't mean it, not for real. There was no reason in the world for me to love her. It was just my brain ordering me to love her. It was not strong enough to make me give in to her plans.

"My cravings are coming back," she told me, touching the lower section of her abdomen, just below her belly button. "I want you to feed me."

I looked at her and shook my head. "No, I don't have to do that."

"But I'm craving you," she said, in as whiny a voice as her dead tone could muster.

"The courts said that I don't have to feed you this month," I said. "It's not the end of the month yet."

"I know you don't have to," she said. "Do it anyway. Do it because you love me."

I could see right through her game and it wasn't going to work. She thought I was compliant and easily manipulated in my blissed-out mental state, but no amount of bliss would make me forget my survival instincts.

"Just a few more days," I said. "Just hold out a few more days."

"I get cranky when I'm hungry," she said.

I rolled my eyes. "Like I can tell the difference..."

CHAPTER TWENTY-TWO

Dokura starved me of her breast milk to get back at me for starving her of my nutrients, so within a couple of days my head cleared up. I felt less lethargic and more energized. After being cooped up in the nest for so long, I decided to go for a walk.

Out in the woods, I spotted a group of women running through the trees. Usagi women in raggedy clothes crept through the bushes like wild animals. They reminded me of Dokura when I'd first met her: sex-crazed wallet-stealing junkies.

When the women saw me, their eyes locked on target. Then they attacked. They charged me from all directions. Now the size of a pre-teen, I couldn't fight back as they grabbed me and pulled me to the ground.

"Wait a minute," I yelled.

I recognized them right away. They were Dokura's sisters. After they had me pinned down, one of them tried to mount me, as if she wanted to have sex with me. I couldn't afford to impregnate more than one Usagi woman, so I tried to fight her off with all of my strength.

"It's me," I said. "Don't you recognize me?"

They pushed away the girl on top of me and then clawed at each other, hissing. One of them was thrown to the ground. Another was slammed against a tree trunk. As the group of women fought, somebody grabbed me from behind.

The strongest of them jumped on top of me and licked my neck. She pulled up my spandex shirt and rubbed her belly toward my penis. As she hungrily stared me in the eyes, I noticed that it was my fluffer from the wedding ceremony. I had no idea how I recognized her out of all the identical twin sisters, but it was definitely her.

She noticed the brand on my chest and froze. It was as if she recognized the imprint of Dokura's vagina. She sniffed at my face, and hands and crotch, then jerked away from me as if she smelled something she didn't like. All of the women scurried over to me one at a time, sniffed at me, and then took off running. I was left lying alone in dead pine needles, battered and wet with saliva.

When I got back to the nest, I asked Dokura what that was all about.

"They were ovulating," Dokura said. "Usagi women get that way at that time of the month. Their cravings make them so ravenous that they become mindless and predatory, like wild animals."

"Like how you were when we first met?"

"Yes," she said. "That rest stop where we met is one of our prime hunting grounds. It was built by my people specifically to lure potential mates. Usagi women with the ravenous hunger will lie in wait within the woods overlooking the area, watching for a lone male that their bodies find appetizing."

"What do you mean their bodies find appetizing?"

"If a male has incompatible DNA or has already begun the mating process with another Usagi female, our bodies will not find him appetizing. But when in the presence of an appetizing male, our pussies will burn and salivate for him. The hunger becomes so overwhelming that we just have to feed. This is how we hunt for males that come from outside of our community. The males inside our community are assigned a mate at a young age."

"So I'm like wild game and they're more like livestock? You grow them yourselves to eat later on?"

"We grow them to become fathers," she said.

"What about the Usagi priest who married us?" I asked. "How come he was never absorbed?"

"No woman ever found him appetizing," she said. "There's either something wrong with his DNA or he is sterile. It happens once every few generations. That Usagi is always made the priest."

"By the way," I said to Dokura. "Why are the Usagi so openly sexual with each other?"

As I asked, I was watching Mrs. Silivasi and another Usagi woman making out on a porch outside the window.

"Our wedding was more debaucherous than any orgy I had ever attended," I said.

"That's because weddings are joyous occasions."

"There are other ways to express joy than kissing and groping," I said.

"Not for the Usagi," she said.

She rubbed her eyes and stared into me.

"You believe Usagi have no emotions, but we do," she said. "We are just incapable of expressing them. The only time we are capable of expressing our emotions is when we are sexually aroused. We communicate our feelings through sexual stimulation."

"It must be frustrating for the men to be constantly aroused," I said, "yet knowing full well that sex will kill them."

"It is part of our culture to relentlessly tease the young Usagi men with sexual stimulation," she said. "The future of our people depends on their willingness to give in to their sexual desires, so Usagi women do everything they can to fill them with lust. From the clothes we wear to the way we look at them, we're constantly seducing them until they finally give in to the mating process. Unfortunately, there are never enough Usagi men to go around. That's why a lot of us have to hunt down our mates from your society."

"How many men from my society end up as Usagi mates?"

"Maybe a thousand a year," she said, "if you count all the Usagi tribes all over the world."

"A thousand? Are you serious?"

"A decade ago it was only a few hundred a year," she said,

"but our population grows quickly due to the size of our litters. It will one day be hundreds of thousands."

"You won't be able to hide your existence from the general public if it keeps going that way."

"By that time, we hope the Usagi will outnumber your people. We believe that by the next millennium all people on the planet will be Usagi."

"So you plan to fuck the normal humans out of existence?"

Kind of like how she planned to fuck me out of existence.

"We don't particularly want it to happen," she said. "It is just bound to happen. We reproduce faster and our genes are stronger."

She was probably correct about that, but only if my people allowed it to happen. They would likely find a reason to wipe out the Usagi long before that ever became a concern.

CHAPTER TWENTY-THREE

When the month was up, Dave didn't show. I had to call him myself, from the pay phone at the rest area. I kept seeing Dokura's rabid sisters lurking in the trees around me as I dialed the phone. I hoped they wouldn't accidentally attack me again.

"Bad news and good news," Dave said when he picked up the phone.

"Okay?"

"Bad news is my people still haven't found an alternate solution to your problem. Good news is I got us an extension."

"What kind of extension?"

"You're going to have to stay there another month," he said.

"Another month? I can't stay here another month."

"And you're going to have to let your wife feed on you," he said.

"Are you fucking with me?"

"Just twice," he said. "That was the deal of the extension. One feeding you'll have to execute immediately. The other can wait a few weeks."

"But who knows how small I'll be after two more feedings?"

"Better small than dead, right? It was the best I could do. Has your wife been breastfeeding you?"

"Yeah, thanks to you. I thought you were going to send food to me."

"I did," he said. "But there were complications. I sent people out there on two different occasions and neither of them came back. We think the Usagi nabbed them. They're denying it, of course. If you see any sign of them you let me know, okay?"

"Sure..." I said.

"As I was saying, you'll have to survive on your wife's milk for a while. That was another part of the agreement."

"It sounds like you're not getting me out of this mess at all, Dave."

"It's just a temporary setback," he said. "I'll make sure you don't...go all the way. One more month, I promise."

After I slammed the phone on the hook, I stormed up the road, furious with Dave's progress. I couldn't believe I had to stay another month with Dokura. I couldn't believe I would be shortened even more.

But even through my fury, a part of me couldn't wait to get back to my nest. A part of me desired to feed her again. It felt good knowing that I didn't have to fight this urge anymore. I could give in to it, just a couple more times.

By the time I saw the Usagi houses on the top of the hill, I found myself running up toward my nest with a giant smile on my face. It was a weird sensation and I truly felt as if my emotions were out of my control, but at that moment I couldn't wait to submit to Dokura's feeding time and let her have at me like an all-you-can-eat buffet.

Dokura lay fat and happy in her nest after having fed on me for over an hour. She rubbed her swollen stomach as I lay against her, weakened and shrunk. I didn't lose much height—maybe an inch at most—but I felt a lot thinner and shriveled. The sex was juicy and divine, but only a few minutes after it was over I wondered if it was worth the loss of flesh. Part of me thought it was.

"We need to do that more often," Dokura said to me. "I should be absorbing about five pounds a week."

"My lawyer said I only have to feed you one more time during the rest of the month," I said.

She lay in silence for a few minutes, listening to the digestive sounds in her stomach.

"No matter how many times you plan to feed me, I need to consume fifteen more pounds of you. We can either spread that out over several small feedings or I will take it in all at one time. What would you rather do?"

"You can control the amount you absorb from me?" I asked.

She nodded. "Just as much as you can control your portion sizes when you eat. I'm more likely to overeat when I've been starved for a while, so it's better to feed me small amounts on a regular schedule. You'll last a lot longer that way."

"So you're saying the more sex we have the less of me you'll absorb in the long run?"

"Exactly."

I thought it over. Losing less mass by having more sex sounded too good to be true. Part of me wondered if she was just telling me what I wanted to hear so that she could eat as much of me as she wanted, whenever she wanted.

"You're not trying to trick me are you?" I asked.

"Of course not," she said, rubbing my thigh. "I love you."

I wasn't entirely convinced, but found myself agreeing to feed her on a regular schedule anyway. I really wished I had a scale to weigh myself, to keep track of the portions she was consuming. Fifteen pounds wasn't too much weight to give up, but I worried she would take advantage of the situation. I didn't want to find myself fifty pounds smaller by the end of the month.

CHAPTER TWENTY-FOUR

We had sex every two days from that point on and she breastfed me up to three times a day. Her milk kept me in a cloudy, blissful state. I felt my body grow addicted to its effects, until I was physically dependent. I got angry and nervous whenever I went too long without her milk. The taste seemed to get better every time I had it. At first, it was too weird and funky, then it was too rich, then it was too sweet. But it quickly became the best-tasting food imaginable. The thought of normal food began to lose its appeal.

Whenever we made love, I couldn't tell that my size was decreasing. I wasn't sure if it was because she was ingesting only small imperceptible amounts of me each time or if I was just so doped up all the time that I didn't recognize any change.

I lay against her staring up at her swollen breasts, which seemed to get bigger by the day. The nipples glistened with moisture. I imagined droplets of milk seeping across those puffy coffee-colored areolas, trickling slowly down the curves of her pale flesh like beads of sweat, then wetting my lips.

Dokura had bulked up a lot lately and for some reason her massiveness aroused me. I wanted to see her get even bigger, curvier. I wanted her to become a voluptuous goddess. I wanted to be wrapped up in her soft ocean of flesh.

Although enraptured by my giant sexy wife, I still wasn't willing to give up my life for her. Dave was going to come through for me. I knew he was. But while I waited for him to find a solution to all of this, I planned to fully enjoy the sensuality of my situation. Every day I had left in that nest I planned to indulge myself, basking in the warmth of my goddess's heavenly flesh.

Dokura inspected her body, touching the excess flesh, as if she was dissatisfied with her current figure. As if she preferred her more slender pre-pregnancy shape.

"I'm glad you weren't a big hefty guy," she told me, examining her plump arm against my small, thin arm. "It would have added way too much extra weight to my body."

I caressed her curvy hips to show her how much I liked her extra padding.

"I would have left the nest looking like a fat slob. Then I'd have to spend months on an exercise regime to burn off all of those extra calories."

A few minutes after she said that, a thought popped into my head. Then my stupid, blissful smile fell from my face.

"Wait a minute..." I said. "If I happened to be a big hefty guy...and you didn't want all of those extra calories making you fat...then why absorb all of me?"

She looked at me with a confused face.

I continued, "You could just absorb the amount of mass that you needed and let the rest of me live on."

"No, I'd have to absorb you all the way."

"Why?"

"That's how it works."

"Would it harm the babies?"

"No, not really. Not if I got enough nutrients."

"Then why absorb me all the way? Why not let me live?"

She didn't answer.

I sat up, excitedly. A brilliant idea popped into my head.

"Actually, even though I'm not a big hefty guy you can still let me live," I said.

I wasn't completely serious about this idea, but it sounded like the perfect backup plan just in case Dave didn't come through for me.

"Why not save just some of me?" I said. "Just a tiny little bit. Even if I were just two inches tall at least I would still be able to survive."

She shook her head sternly. "No, I have to absorb you all the way."

"But why?"

"Because..."

She paused for a moment.

"Because that's the best part."

"What is?" I asked.

"Once you're small enough to swallow whole. That's the best part of the mating process."

"Even if it's not necessary?"

"It's like when you're eating a really good meal and save the best bite for last," she said. "You can't just throw away the best bite. That's what you were looking forward to the whole time."

"So it's not because of necessity? It's just for pleasure?"

"It's both."

"But you're asking me to give up my life. Not for the children as I thought, but so that you can fully enjoy your mating process." I scooted away from her toward the edge of the nest. "You say that you love me. If you loved me, wouldn't you want to keep me alive? Even if I were small?"

"I don't know."

"What if I weighed four hundred pounds when we met? Would you let me live then?"

"But you didn't weigh four hundred pounds. You weighed two hundred pounds at most. I need all two hundred pounds."

"You can save just a tiny bit. One pound? Six ounces? One ounce? There's got to be some small sacrifice you'd be willing to make."

"What would be the point of staying alive if you were that small?"

"It's better than dying."

"But you wouldn't be any use to me or the children," she said. "I would rather swallow you."

"I could probably still use the internet and do my job online," I said. "It might take a while to type on a keyboard the size of a basketball court, but I could earn a good amount of money for the family."

She shook her head. "I would rather swallow you."

"Even though you love me?"

"I would do it because I love you."

"No, you would do it for pleasure."

"I don't care why I'd do it. I want my last bite."

"You're selfish."

"I want my last bite."

Although she had her usual emotionless Vulcan face on, she appeared to be pouting.

"Your mom was right when she said you were gluttonous," I said.

"No, I'm not."

"You even said so yourself."

"If I were really gluttonous you'd be all gone by now."

After that, she didn't speak to me for the rest of the day. I wasn't even allowed to sleep next to her until I promised never to bring that topic up ever again. I realized it would have been hopeless to try to convince her anyway. Her Usagi instincts probably made it impossible to do as I asked. Every fiber of her being was probably screaming at her to consume me. Not just a part of me, but every last drop of me.

I knew because I was feeling it, too. Every fiber of my being was screaming at me to let her consume me. When we were about to make love, the thought of sex wasn't turning me on. It was the thought of being consumed by her that made me erect. I also understood why Dokura absolutely needed to have her last bite. I also felt it. When she fed on me, taking in a little of my mass at a time, it seemed like just a tease. It seemed like the only point to that was just to make me smaller, so that at some point I would become small enough to fit all the way inside. If my will to live wasn't so strong, I would have been longing for that day just as much as she was.

I hoped Dave would get me out of there soon. Just as a guy finds it harder to stop having sex the closer he comes to orgasm, I believed that the smaller Dokura made me the harder it was going to be to resist going all the way.

CHAPTER TWENTY-FIVE

The days blurred together. I couldn't tell night from day. It was all just a drugged-up haze of sleeping, snuggling, sexing, and sucking on a bed of breasts. Dokura, myself, and our nest all seemed to ooze together into one life form. Sometimes, I couldn't figure out which one was me.

One day, I awoke from blissful cozy dreams to the annoying sound of my mother's voice entering our house.

She danced toward us, singing her words as she said, "Look at the little love birds, snuggling in their love nest!"

Then she hugged both of us at once through the covers.

"Oh, don't the two of you look so cute in there!" she said. "You're all bundled up like baby bunnies."

She stroked the outside of our covers as if she were petting us. I tried to just ignore her and go back to sleep.

"Sorry I haven't been visiting you two," she said. "But I've got a new life coach who has been helping me decorate my sun room. We're turning it into a yoga and meditation studio with bamboo paneling and Tuscan-style ambient lighting. It's very feng shui. You wouldn't believe how much it's changed my life. The man is a godsend."

I really wished she would just shut up and go away.

"We're sleeping, Mom," I said.

"Oh, you can take a break for a while to have a quick visit with your mother," she said. "You're not going to be around forever, you know."

She pulled the blankets off us. I quickly grabbed them to cover at least the lower half of my body.

"Let me get a good look at the two of you." She looked at Dokura. "You're looking nice and healthy. And big too! Look at your belly!"

I sat up and shook my head to sober myself. As my mother

put her paws all over my wife's belly, I realized that it did look pretty big. Not because she was full of my flesh, either. She looked really pregnant. Several-babies pregnant.

"And you!" she said when she saw me.

She let go of Dokura's body and came around to the front of the bed to examine me more closely.

"Wow," said my mother, "she's really been wolfing you down, hasn't she? Look at how little you are! You're hardly a full meal anymore!"

I looked down at my body. I didn't feel much smaller. Maybe ten or twenty pounds lighter, but no big deal.

My mother elbowed me jokingly. "When I said I wanted you to fatten her up, I didn't mean feed her all of you at once." Then she giggled. "Save some of you for dessert!"

"You're really getting a kick out of all of this, aren't you?" I said.

"Oh, I'm just joshing with you," said my mom. "You know that's how I cope."

She sat down on the bed next to me.

"Look," she said, trying to get serious. "I'm really proud of you for going through with this. You're doing the right thing." Then she tilted her head to the side. "I know you think your publishing work is incredibly important, but it's really not significant in the grand scheme of things. Nothing is more important than having children. There's absolutely nothing that a parent shouldn't be willing to sacrifice for their sake." She wiped a tear away from her eye. "Even if you have to give up your own life."

I shook my head at her and said, "I'm not going through with it. Dave is still going to get me out of this. You just watch."

"Oh, yeah right," she said, rolling her teary eyes. "Just give it up already and accept your fate. You're the only thing that can give your babies the proper nutrition that they require. For an Usagi like you, it's the natural order of things."

"But I'm not an Usagi."

"Oh, grow up," said my mother. "You became an Usagi the

second you knocked up an Usagi. There's no turning back now. Your family needs you."

"But I don't need my family!"

Tears flooded my mother's eyes.

"Why are you doing this to me?" my mother said. "Don't you know how hard this is for me? I'm trying to look at this as a beautiful, positive thing, but you keep trying to make me see it as something monstrous and cruel."

"It is monstrous and cruel."

"Only if you look at it that way it is," she said.

Then my mother began to cry. I had to apologize and calm her down. It was very typical of her. Whenever I had an emotional problem, she would always figure out a way to turn the conversation around to make it all about her. I always ended up comforting her when I was the one who needed to be comforted.

My mother continued, "But you can also see this as beautiful. You will become one with your wife and then give birth to a whole litter of children. If this were normal and everyone in the world reproduced like the Usagi you wouldn't think of it as such a bad thing. Like growing old and dying, it is the natural cycle of life."

"You're right, you're right," I said. "I'll try to see it as something beautiful, as you say."

She was full of shit, but I wanted to make peace. Arguing with her never got me anywhere.

Dokura and my mother had a long talk about absolutely nothing. It was mostly my mother talking. Dokura didn't say anything unless she was answering a question. I just sat there, trying to tune them out.

"Moochy, moochy!" my mother said, trying to get my attention. "Look, look!"

She laughed her ass off for a minute and then shifted Dokura toward me so that I could see what she had done.

"Look what I drew!" she said.

On Dokura's pregnant belly, with a sharpie pen, my mother had drawn a wacky happy face. She cracked up when I saw it, but I wasn't laughing with her. Neither was Dokura.

"Watch, watch this, watch," she said, and then she shook Dokura's naked belly to make the drawing's mouth move.

Making the voice of a cutesy cartoon fat guy, my mother acted as if the belly was speaking to me.

"Hi there, moochy," she made it say, "I'm Dokura's belly. How are you doing there, little guy?"

Then she giggled wildly. I shook my head and looked away.

"I'm having a hankerin' for somethin' tasty," she continued. "What's on the menu today? Oh, it's moochy again! My favorite dish! Mmmmmm, he'll be nummy in my tummy!"

I fought the urge to strangle her to death right then and there.

"Come on, get in my belly!" she made it say. Then she laughed louder than ever. "Hey, moochy! Remember Fat Bastard from Austin Powers?" She tried to impersonate Fat Bastard from Austin Powers while jiggling Dokura's stomach. "Get in my belly! Get in my belly!"

I really, really, really fought the urge to strangle her to death right then and there.

"Pretend you're Mini-Me!" said my mom. "You know, from Austin Powers!"

I looked up at Dokura and said, "Why are you letting her get away with that?"

Dokura just stared at me blankly. "She's having fun. I like it."

I groaned loudly. Dokura was a perfect daughter-in-law for my mother—a woman who was completely malleable.

My mom cackled. "Get in my belly! Get in my belly!"

When my mother was finally leaving, I couldn't have been happier. I wanted to rejoin Dokura in the warm nest and go back into blissful dream worlds.

My mother kissed me goodbye.

"Bye sweetie," she said. "I'll try to visit more often. I'm thinking about maybe getting a studio in the area. Or maybe a summer cottage. Wouldn't that be fun for me? Living so close to my grandkids!"

I tried pushing away her hugs but she was way too strong for my diminished body.

"Make sure Dokura rations you out more," she said, hugging me close. "You want to last long enough to become plenty of nourishing milk for my hungry little grandbabies."

A part of me wanted to tell her to go fuck herself, but I found myself reacting obediently. As if she had just told me to do my homework or clean my room.

"Okay, Mom," I said. "I'll do that."

I wasn't sure if it was because I wanted to be agreeable just to get rid of her or because a part of me knew that what she said was something I should be doing even if I didn't want to do it.

"Bye my darlings," she said, hugging both myself and Dokura at the same time. "Now you two love birds go back to nesting. You're so cute together!"

After she left, I suddenly didn't feel much like nesting. The mood was lost.

I crawled out of bed and nearly fell on my face trying to walk on my legs. I couldn't remember when I'd last left the bed. For some reason, I didn't need to use the bathroom as much. Perhaps the breast milk didn't create a lot of waste. In the bathroom, my penis discharged a thick languid stream into the pit below the toilet seat. It wasn't just urine, but urine mixed with semen and other pinkish goop. Perhaps some of my liquefied mass had been left behind in my shaft after the last feeding. For some reason, that thought made me stop urinating. My urethral sphincter locked up, as if trying to hold the goop inside, not wanting to waste it.

When I left the bathroom, Dokura stood at the foot of the bed.

"Come to me," she said. "I want a taste of you. Just a little snack."

I found myself obediently stepping toward her. As I neared her and looked up at her glowing eyes staring down on me, I realized just how enormous she had become. As I wrapped my arms around her, I found my face in her pubic hair. That was when I finally realized my size. I was the height of a five-year-old child.

"Why am I so small?" I said, pushing myself away from her.

She stepped toward me and I stepped back.

"Because I've been feeding," she said, gripping the sides of her massive stomach, which all of a sudden seemed twice my size.

"You said you'd only take five pounds of me per week," I said. "Look at how much you've taken. I knew I shouldn't have trusted you."

"What do you mean?" she said. "I have only been taking five pounds of you per week. Actually, I've been taking less than that."

"Then why am I so short?" I asked. "I should only be fifteen pounds lighter."

She looked at me for a moment, as if searching for a response.

"But we made that agreement over three months ago," she said.

I thought about it for a minute and then shook my head frantically.

"No," I said. "It's only been a few weeks."

"Look at me," she said, holding her belly. "Our babies wouldn't have grown this much in only three weeks."

I tried to remember. I knew I had been in a blissed-out stupor for quite a while, but had I really lost track of that much time? It didn't seem possible.

"But why..." I couldn't form words. "Why didn't I know..."

She wanted to comfort me but I pulled away.

"Time is hard to calculate when nesting," she said. "It is a beautiful part of the mating process. Time becomes irrelevant. It seems to fly by yet also slows down to the point where it feels like it will last forever."

"But why didn't Dave come back?" I asked. "There was supposed to be a trial. He was supposed to get me out of this by now."

She didn't know how to respond to that.

I went for my spandex clothes lying on the wooden floor, covered in shriveled long-dead flower petals. The pants were too big, so I had to wear the shirt like a dress.

"Where do you think you're going?" she asked.

"I need to call Dave," I said, tying my too-big shoes to my feet.

"But what about my snack?" she asked.

"Fuck your snack," I said.

Then I stormed out of the house, leaving her standing naked by the bed.

CHAPTER TWENTY-SIX

I hiked into the forest and down the hill toward the rest stop. It was the middle of spring and the sun was shining so bright that I could hardly see. My shadow was huge behind me, following me like a phantom reaper coming to collect my soul.

The trip took forever, as if walking on short child-sized legs made the distance twice as far. I also lacked energy and quickly became agitated from being deprived of Dokura's milk for so long. I didn't remember the last time I had some.

It took a couple hours before I was able to get Dave on the phone. He seemed surprised to hear from me.

"What the hell happened?" I yelled. "How could you abandon me like that?"

"Oh..." Dave said.

It took a lot of shouting before I could get him to explain himself.

"Were you just fucking with me the whole time?" I asked. "Did you give up on me or was there ever actually going to be a trial at all?"

He sighed. Then he apologized, his voice full of guilt and empathy. I couldn't tell if it was genuine or if he was just putting on his best lawyer act.

"There was a trial a long time ago," he told me. "In fact, it took place only a couple of weeks after your wedding."

"What? It was before the last time we spoke?"

"I was sure I could get you off," he said. "I knew I had it in my power to save you."

"Then what the hell happened? You couldn't find an alternate solution?"

"Actually, I found multiple solutions to your problem," he said. "It didn't take long at all. A research team took in an Usagi volunteer. Within just a matter of days they had figured out multiple ways to save you that would not harm the development of the children."

"Then why am I still here?"

"The court ruled against you," he said. "They were worried the alternate solutions I presented would harm the children. Even though I had all the proof they would ever need that the children would be born just as healthy using these methods, none of them thought it was worth the risk."

"How could they do that?" I asked. "This is my life that's on the line."

"You have to understand," he said. "A lot of these people were offended by the fact that you were unwilling to make the sacrifice for your children. They made you out to be the absolute worst kind of human being—someone who puts themselves above their children. The reason they ruled against you was because they wanted you to go through with it, even though you didn't need to. They wanted to make an example of you."

"It's easy for them to say. They're not in my shoes. They don't have to sacrifice what I have to sacrifice."

"Actually, they all decided that they would have gladly given up their lives if they were in your shoes. Maybe they wouldn't if they had an alternate solution, but they would have done whatever it took to make sure their children were born healthy and strong."

"They're full of shit," I said.

I stewed for a moment, too angry to speak.

"Why didn't you tell me any of this sooner?" I asked him. "Why did you say the trial date had been postponed and then leave me hanging?"

He was silent for a moment. I could hear him tapping a pen against his desk.

"I did that for your sake," he said. "Once I knew there was no way out for you, I told you to start drinking the Usagi milk. I knew that its effects would make you want to go through with the assimilation. I figured it would be best if you decided to stay with your wife, rather than tell you that you had no choice but to stay with her. It was unfair, I know, but if I were in your shoes that's how I would have wanted it to happen."

"All you did was give me false hope," I said.

"I guess I made a mistake," he said. "I'm sorry."

He screwed me. The one person I thought I could count on screwed me. Had he been honest from the start I would have figured another way out.

"I'm not going to give in," I told him. "I'm not going to just lie down and die."

"It's over," he said. "There's no way out of this."

"But I have to try."

"And what would you do?" he said. "Even if you could escape from the Usagi, what then? You'd be a fugitive. Everyone on this planet would be against you. Even your family would be against you. I sure as hell wouldn't risk my career to help you. You'd just get caught and brought right back. And if they didn't catch you right away you'd end up killing your children."

"I don't care," I said. "Fuck the children. Do you hear me? Fuck them! What are they even going to amount to anyway? I'm the best damned editor in the publishing industry. I'm one in a million. All that those kids are going to do with their worthless Usagi lives is sit in the woods staring at each other, have kids of their own, then die. And then those kids will do the same goddamned thing. As will their kids. My life actually has meaning. I'm worth a hundred of them!"

"Get off your high horse, asshole." Dave lost his sympathetic tone. "What makes you so goddamned special? You're a book editor. Big fucking deal. It's just a job. I'm the best lawyer I know. But do I think my life is worth more than anyone else's because of that? No. You might as well be the best damned janitor on the planet. It doesn't mean anything."

"But I bring works of art into the world," I said. "I help writers achieve their dreams. Those writers, those books—they are my children. And they are better than children. They are immortal. They bring hope and happiness and meaning to the world."

Dave tried to speak but I cut him off, raising my voice

even louder. "What if Vincent van Gogh gave up his art to have children? What if Beethoven was gobbled up by some Usagi bitch's cunt before he could make symphonies? What if Shakespeare sacrificed his future for the sake of his kids? The world doesn't need more kids. It needs more Shakespeares. More Beethovens. And it needs me. I might just be an editor, but without people like me there would be no Shakespeares. There would be no Twains or Faulkners or Stephen Fucking Kings. So I can't just give up. I can't die. Not for my children, not for anyone. I have to continue my work."

There was a silence on the other end. For a minute, I thought he had hung up on me.

"Look," Dave said. "It doesn't matter anyway. Even if you escaped and moved to Canada, even if you won the trial, even if you never met the Usagi girl in the first place, you still wouldn't be able to continue your work. Your boss would have laid you off."

"What are you talking about?"

"The publishing industry is changing rapidly," he said. "The government is getting involved. Like they did with film and television a few years ago, they won't allow any books to be published unless they are family-friendly. Even classic works of literature that aren't kid-friendly will be either censored, altered, or banned from print. Editors now have to be approved by government officials. With the kinds of books you've released throughout your career, there's no way you would ever work in the industry again."

Rage boiled inside me. I couldn't even speak.

"So, you're wrong," Dave continued. "The world doesn't need you. There is no future for you in the publishing industry and everything you accomplished meant nothing in the grand scheme of things. Every book you've ever gotten published will be taken out of print, pulled from the shelves, and forgotten. You're just as insignificant as the rest of us."

I didn't want to believe him. It couldn't be true. I wanted to put my hand through the phone and rip his throat out for telling such lies.

"Go home to your wife," he said. "She needs you more than the world does. I'm sorry I couldn't save you, but it was beyond my control. I guess this was what life had in store for you."

He let out a long sigh. It was his way of saying goodbye to me.

"Don't worry about my bill," he said, just before he hung up. "Your mother already took care of it."

I kept the phone held up to my ear long after the dial tone went dead. The next thing I knew I was back in the nest with Dokura, drinking milk from her breast. It wasn't fair what was happening to me. None of it was fair.

CHAPTER TWENTY-SEVEN

As I lay in bed next to my giant snoring blob of a wife, I decided that I had to get out of there. I didn't care about what Dave had said. He could have been lying. And even if he wasn't lying that didn't mean I should just give up. The fact that the future of literature was in jeopardy meant that I was needed more than ever. I had to stop it from happening. If they wouldn't let me work in New York I would move to a different country with a more liberal government. I would publish English books that could be sold in the American underground. No, I couldn't just let myself die. I had to survive. I had to fight for the future of the written word.

I thought about ways I could get out of my mess. I could murder Dokura and somehow make it look like an accident. I could chop off my own penis so that she had no way of absorbing me. There had to be any number of ways I could get out of this. I just had to be creative.

Then I noticed something missing from my ankle. The device that the policeman attached to my leg the day Dave took my case was no longer there. I looked around the room and saw it lying on the floor by the edge of the nest. It must have fallen off a long time ago and I hadn't noticed in my drugged-up haze. There was nothing stopping me from escaping at that moment. Dokura was sleeping. It was night. All I had to do was get away from there. The babies would be fine. If I went missing, the courts would have no choice but to use Dave's alternate methods to keep her children alive. Perhaps that would save several other men like me from the Usagi in the future.

Before I left, I would search the Usagi homes to see if there were any other men being held prisoner. Dave said two delivery boys went missing. They had to have been here somewhere. Together we could team up and get away. One of us was bound to know somebody who could help us escape the country. It was a way out. I really had a way out.

I stepped out of the bed, slipped on the spandex shirt, and crept across the hardwood floor. Then I looked back. The warm blob of woman was fast asleep. She wouldn't know I was gone until morning. Taking a deep breath, I opened the door and stepped out into the night.

It was cold. My exposed legs quivered as the wind hit them. The Usagi houses were huge and dark. I had no idea where the other men could be kept prisoner. The last thing I wanted to do was wake any of the sleeping residents of the homes. I decided that it might be best to just get out on my own.

As I stepped toward the woods, I noticed how dark it was out there. There wasn't a moon out that night, so I couldn't see a thing. And it was so cold. And lonely.

I looked back at my home. It looked warm and safe. The thought of leaving Dokura suddenly filled me with anxiety. I imagined how she would feel if she woke up and realized I was gone forever. Even though she couldn't express emotion, she could still feel it. She would be so devastated. I didn't want to do that to her. I wanted her to be happy. All I wanted to do was be with her and hold her and let her swallow me alive with her vagina and digest me to feed our babies.

I shook my head violently, realizing that those thoughts weren't mine. They were programmed into my head. I didn't really want any of that. Dokura didn't give a shit about me. I didn't give a shit about her. She was a fat fucking parasitic blob who was only using me. I owed her nothing.

Looking back at the forest, I decided I had to do it. I had to escape. No matter how cold or dark. I would find a way to safety. I would survive and make the most of the rest of my life. My will was strong.

But my feet wouldn't move. My mind told me to flee, but my body refused. The next thing I knew I was running back to my home and crawling into bed with Dokura.

The second she saw me, her eyes glowing in the dark beneath the covers, she said, "I'm starving."

Just by hearing those two little words, I felt myself become instantly erect. She got on top of me and put my penis inside her, careful not to crush my tiny frame. I shivered at the sight of the sharpie smiley face as her massive stomach oozed on top of me, covering my body up to my neck.

I cried as she fucked me, tears pouring down my cheeks onto her belly. It was at that moment that I realized I wasn't getting out of there. I was destined to be food for my family, just as everyone in the world wanted me to be. There was no escape. My will had been broken. And the worst part, the reason why I was bawling like I had never bawled before, was that all I could think about was how I would rather be there in that moment, feeding myself to Dokura, than anywhere else in the world.

The days melted slowly together as I melted slowly into my wife. Sex was becoming stranger and stranger the smaller I became. She was like an avalanche of flesh that buried me whenever she was hungry. Because she had control of her vaginal muscles, she was able to constrict her labia around my penis so that the feeling was not lost no matter how tiny my member became. It wasn't long before I was so small that Dokura could have easily smothered me to death if she wasn't careful.

As the delivery date neared, she was a grotesque human beached whale with swollen drippy teats. Her belly, pregnant with so many shifting squirming babies, was larger than the rest of her body. She could no longer leave the bed, even if she needed to. Just rolling over to feed on me was too much for her. I had to climb the mountain of her pale sweaty meat to feed her from above, or sometimes I would squeeze my way through folds of flesh beneath her stomach to reach the hungry, waiting, lower mouth. This would have been disgusting to the old me, but nothing about Dokura disgusted me anymore. Even the grossest, smelliest, most mutated aspects of her deformed body turned me on.

I no longer cared about escape. Life outside of the nest seemed meaningless. My old life, the publishing industry, the future of literature; none of it mattered anymore. I just wanted to feed Dokura. And I longed for the day when I could finally be fully absorbed by her body.

"What is the blob?" Dokura asked me one day.

Her flesh was folded around me like a blanket.

"Huh?"

She lifted a mound of belly to look at me below her.

"You called me the blob on our wedding night," she said. "I wondered what a blob was."

"It is a creature that wraps itself around its prey and digests it alive," I said. "The more it consumes the larger it becomes."

"Oh," she said, "like me."

Then she thought about it for a while.

"Is the blob sexy?" she asked.

"Well, it's formless goo that oozes from place to place. I'm not sure if that can be considered sexy."

"Oh," she said. "I don't want to be the blob unless it is sexy."

"Well..." I rubbed her blob-like flesh. "You're the sexiest blob I've ever met."

She closed her eyes and relaxed her muscles, her blubbery stomach oozing over me like a sexy formless blob.

When it came time for the children to be born, I observed with amazement from the edge of the nest as the tiny chubby creatures seeped out of her in gooey balls. They didn't look like human babies. They were kind of grub-like, similar to insect larvae. Their mouths were low on their faces. Their eyes were the size of golf balls and inky blue in color. They did not cry. They crawled on their own immediately to Dokura's breasts. The sight of them filled my soul with warmth. They were miracles, all of them.

I cried with guilt when I realized that if the old me had his way, none of them would be here now. I thought about how horrible I was. I just didn't understand. I was selfish. Everyone else knew better than I did. They all knew that I needed to do the right thing. And I thanked the heavens that I eventually came to my senses and decided to go through with it in the end.

There was only sixteen pounds of me left. I prayed it was going to be enough to last Dokura through the early critical nursing period before she was able to leave the nest. I wished more than anything that I could have been a larger man, one who could have provided more nutrients than my family could ever need.

When the babies were all born, all nine of them sucking at Dokura's teats, I smiled with tears running down my eyes. I wanted to join my family in their cuddling mass and nurse with them, but Dokura pushed me away with her foot when I tried to get close.

"You're not allowed to drink from me for a few days," she said. "The babies need the milk more than you right now."

"Then I should just starve?" I asked.

"I have something else that will nourish you."

As she closed her eyes and squeezed it out, I realized what she had in mind.

It was my job to eat the afterbirth.

CHAPTER TWENTY-EIGHT

Without the milk for a few days, I went through withdrawal. When I finally drank it again, I realized it had completely lost its potency. Her body was no longer producing the chemicals that made me drunk and docile. The milk was now designed for the babies. It did nothing but keep me fed. My brain sobered and I found my situation much less pleasurable than I had before.

The babies did not take to me very well once I had shrunk to their height. They were bigger than me in mass. I was about the same height as they were, but they had twice the weight. They were chubby and broad. Whenever I tried to feed on Dokura, they pushed and kicked me away from her nipples. They saw me as competition for the milk. I didn't belong.

"Oh, look at the little darlings suckling at their momma's teats!" my mother said on her next visit. "They're like little piglets! Nana's little piggies!"

Dokura glared at my mother when she tried to pick up one of the babies attached to her nipples. Her glowing eyes said, "Do not fuck with me or my children." Even though my mother had more nerve than anyone I'd ever known, just one look from Dokura and she was instantly put in her place.

So my mother turned her attention to me. She picked me up like a baby and spun me around in her arms.

"Oh, look at my cute little moochy, the size of an iddy biddy baby," she said. "I always wished I had the power to shrink you down to the size of a baby and keep you that way forever. Who'd a thunk my dream would come true!"

I was about to tell her off when she spun me around over the nest like an airplane, nearly making me puke all over the place.

"Weeeeeee!" she cried. "Moochy, you're superbaby! Up, up and away!"

It was like she couldn't tell the difference between a baby and a man that had shrunk to the size of a baby. Once she nearly rammed my skull into the wall from flying me around the room so haphazardly, I yelled at her to stop.

"Oh, who's a little cranky pants," she sang to me in baby-talk, bouncing me in her arms. "Cranky, cranky, cranky pants!"

Then she put her massive face into my belly and gave me a zerbert.

My mother visited almost daily from that point on. She completely lost interest in me once she was able to hold the real babies. The fact that they looked more like alien larvae than human infants did not seem to bother her. They were still the cutest little things in the world.

She bounced one of them in her arms, making coo-kissing noises at it. But Dokura would never let her hold one for longer than a few minutes before demanding it back.

"Go to Mommy," said my mother, as she placed the baby on my wife's stomach.

Dokura's stomach was flat and tight again. Apart from her swollen breasts, her whole body was back in its original shape.

"I can't believe how slender you look after having so many kids," my mother said to Dokura. "Wish I looked that good after giving birth."

Then my mother turned to me.

"Good job keeping her fit, moochy," she said. "You must be low in carbs!"

I really didn't like having my mother around anymore. It seemed to pervert the nesting experience. I completely understood why it was customary for the Usagi to prohibit anyone from disturbing the wedding nest.

Whenever the babies were not nursing, I would take the

opportunity to breastfeed without the competition. But if my mother was around, she would pull me away from my wife's nipples.

"Oh, no you don't, mister!" she cried. "That milk is for the babies. It's going to be wasted on you."

I said, "What should I do, just sit back and starve?"

She replied, "No, what you should do is let Dokura slurp the rest of you up, so her body can turn you into milk for the babies. Don't you think it's about time?"

"It's not up to you," I said. "That's between me and my wife."

"Tell him, Dokura," my mother said. "It's time to polish him off, isn't it?"

Dokura shook her head at my mother.

"I want to save him for a bit longer."

"For how long?" my mother complained. "You have hungry babies to feed!"

"I don't know..." Dokura said.

"You have to do it sooner or later," she said. "There's no time like the present."

"God, Mom!" I said. "It's a private matter. This doesn't concern you."

"If it affects the health of my grandkids then it concerns me," she said. "This is a crucial stage in your babies' development. They need lots of fresh milk."

Dokura looked at me with a soft gaze. She was trying to read my thoughts.

"Maybe we should," she said to me.

"How about tomorrow night?" my mother said. "I'll take your babies next door to your mother's and give you two some privacy."

Dokura and I looked at each other. I didn't like my mother dictating my execution date, but I knew she was right. It just felt like the right time.

"Okay," I said, nodding quietly. "Tomorrow night."

My mother clapped her hands together. "It's settled then."

She turned to my babies and patted each of them on the butt.

"Did you hear that, my piggies?" she said in a baby voice. "Your daddy's going to say bye-bye to fill your tummies. Isn't he the best daddy ever?"

As she kissed each of my children's bare butts, her tone of voice made me feel incredibly nauseous. Just the sight of her made me sick. For some reason, I began to think that everything that had happened to me was all because of her.

I really wasn't going to miss my mother one little bit.

CHAPTER TWENTY-NINE

It is now the last day of my life. I spent the morning snuggling with Dokura and my babies in a big pile. It was the first time my children embraced me and accepted me as a part of the family. Perhaps they knew the sacrifice I planned to make for them. Perhaps they wanted to finally show their appreciation.

"I want to name one of them after you," Dokura said to me.

"Which one?" I asked.

There were two males in the litter.

"That one," she said. "I will call him Moochy."

"Moochy isn't my real name," I said.

"It's not?"

"That's just what my mother calls me."

"Oh..." she said. "Well, I'll call him Moochy anyway. After you."

When my mother and my mother-in-law arrived to take the babies, my mom seemed like she wanted to get in and out of there as quickly as she could. She probably was so excited to have a few hours alone with her grandbabies that she had forgotten this was the last day of my life. But I knew my mother. I knew she hated negativity so much that she just ignored it. It will take a few weeks before she realizes that her son is dead and gone.

Before I saw my mother-in-law for the last time, she said in a very sincere voice, "I want to thank you for your sacrifice. You don't know what it means to my daughter. She had always wanted children of her own. It is because of you that she has become a mother. I thank you from the bottom of my heart for all that you have given us."

Then she pulled out a necklace. It was Dokura's wedding necklace, the one that contained my severed finger. The finger had been bleached in the sun and was now just bone.

"She will wear this piece of you for the rest of her life, to remind her of the great sacrifice you have made for the future of our people."

Mrs. Silivasi set the necklace down on a table and then bowed to me. I bowed my baby-sized body back at her.

Before I saw my real mother for the last time, all she said to me was, "Bye, moochy! I love you!"

Then she waved one of my baby's tiny hands and pretended to speak in a baby voice, "Bye, Daddy! Bye-bye! We'll always love you!"

Just before she closed the door behind her, my mother smiled at Dokura and told her, "Bon appétit!"

I felt a little better knowing that I would never have to see her again.

It is time.

I'm looking up at Dokura's massive frame and she's staring down at me. I can almost see a wicked smile on her face even though her expression is blank. With the Usagi, sometimes you can see their expressions not in their faces but behind their eyes. If I were to have lived with them longer I might have learned how to read their emotions this way.

"I want you to be a four-course meal," she says. "I want to savor you all night."

For the first course, she pulls me on top of her, between her canyon-like legs. And I make love to her until I shrink to the size of a bunny rabbit.

"From behind now," she says.

Her ass is the size of a garbage truck as I stand behind her, feeding Dokura her second course from an angle we never tried while she was pregnant. It excites her so much that she takes in half of my mass. I'm now the size of a Barbie doll.

Dokura wants to do it with her on top now. I have no idea how it can be done without crushing me.

"For the next course," she says. "I want you to get well acquainted with my pussy. It would be good if you got to know her first before she swallows you whole."

I realize what she's going on about once she lowers her crotch toward my body. Her vagina is massive. It is the length of almost half my body. I can see every pore and wrinkle in its flesh. It no longer seems like a part of Dokura. It seems like it is a sentient being of its own.

Looking up at her vagina as if it were my god, I become overwhelmed by its magnitude. I feel powerless and unworthy in its presence. The lips widen and a wave of warmth hits my body like the breath of a dragon. I gaze up into its cavernous maw. It begins to salivate, droplets of moisture oozing against my chest.

The lips close and it kisses my chest. Then it lowers itself and kisses my belly. The mouth opens and sucks on my torso. I raise my hands to it and rub my fingers along the rims. It quivers above me. With my palms coated in moisture, I caress the clitoris. For me, it is the size of a grapefruit. I shift around the globe like I'm looking at the future inside a crystal ball.

Dokura's moans vibrate through her whole body. She lowers herself onto me, wrapping her vaginal lips around me like a juicy blanket. It slides down my torso toward my crotch and sucks the entire region into its mouth. Her shrubbery of pubic hair buries me up to my neck.

My penis is so small that it's not as if she's actually fucking me. She just rubs her vaginal lips against me like two massive tongues. When I come, her lips tighten around my entire lower half and slurp me up. I shrink so quickly that I feel as if it is going to take me all the way in. I grab onto her pubic hair as the vacuum sucks at me, in a desperate attempt to save myself from being swallowed completely. Her lips tug on my lower body, but I refuse to let go. I'm not ready to be devoured quite yet.

I'm only two inches high by the time the sucking stops. Do-kura lifts herself up to her knees and I find myself being pulled up with her. My body is stuck to her labia. Her vaginal juices act as adhesive, keeping me plastered tight to her pubic area. I see her massive fingers open beneath me and then peel me off her lower lips like a soggy Band-Aid.

She brings me up to her face. Those glowing blue eyes like pools of sapphire. Her mouth opens and she sucks on my body, cleaning off the vaginal fluids that coat my skin.

"Are you ready to do the handsome squirm?" she asks.

"The handsome squirm?"

She squeezes my body gently between her fingers and says, "That's what we call it when an Usagi male is completely devoured by his wife's vagina."

I nod my head at her. I have never been more ready for anything in my life.

She brings my body to her mouth and gives me a soft, loving kiss. I find myself hugging her lips like pillows and kissing them with all the passion left in my tiny being. It is our goodbye. No words are necessary.

As she brings my body back down toward the gaping maw of her vagina, she caresses me against a row of her nipples. She squeezes me between two breasts and slides me across her smooth pale stomach. I can hear gurgling noises as I pass over her belly. It is the sound of her body processing the part of me she's already ingested tonight.

She doesn't swallow me all at once. She masturbates with me first, sucks on me, slides me around the edges as if savoring my flavor. Once I am pulled all the way in, all my senses vanish apart from my sense of touch. I feel my body being gulped down a throat-like passage and pulled deep into her moist cavern. It doesn't seem as if I even need to breathe anymore. I'm becoming a part of her.

For some reason, I am still alive. I'm not instantly turned to mush as I'd expected. Her warm flesh is all around me, caressing me, creating tingling feelings. The sensation is incredibly pleasurable. It's familiar, but like nothing I've ever felt before. As the caressing continues, the sensation heightens. I realize what it is. The feeling is the same as when I have sex. Only, instead of being concentrated solely on my penis, this sensation ripples through every inch of my entire body.

I can hear Dokura's moans vibrating all around me. She can feel it, too. We are somehow making love as I'm being digested. My body quivers and I feel Dokura's body pulsing all around me. The sensation intensifies. As I approach orgasm, the mass beneath my skin begins to liquefy. I become like a water balloon, filled with warm soupy fluid. The fluid bubbles inside me and my skin stretches and expands.

Dokura cries out in ecstasy, her climax causing the wet meat around me to shiver like an earthquake. Orgasm invades my every pore. When I ejaculate, my whole body explodes. I pop like a balloon and all of my insides ooze out, splashing against the walls of Dokura's inner digestive cavity.

Even though my body is formless, just a mass of cum-like soup, I still have consciousness for some reason. A sense of peace fills me. I feel myself becoming a part of Dokura. All of a sudden, I can feel what she feels. I can see what she sees.

She is lying in her nest with her hands on her belly, her eyes rolling back in bliss. A glowy, satisfied feeling stretches over her entire body. And just as I can feel her sensations, she too can feel what I am feeling. We are becoming one.

We lie together, basking in each other's flesh, as her body absorbs every last drop of my essence. I never wanted to give up everything for the sake of a family. I never wanted to lose my individuality, give up my future, or sacrifice my happiness for the happiness of others. But as Dokura melts the very last cell of my identity, I realize that individuality is overrated. Humans are designed to merge together, to lose themselves in each other. Relationships, family, civilization—it's all just one big melding, growing, mutating, sexy blob. Who am I to fight against that?

THE END

ABOUT THE AUTHOR

Carlton Mellick III is one of the leading authors of the bizarro fiction subgenre. Since 2001, his books have drawn an international cult following, despite the fact that they have been shunned by most libraries and chain bookstores.

He won the Wonderland Book Award for his novel, *Warrior Wolf Women of the Wasteland*, in 2009. His short fiction has appeared in *Vice Magazine, The Year's Best Fantasy and Horror #16, The Magazine of Bizarro Fiction,* and *Zombies: Encounters with the Hungry Dead*, among others. He is also a graduate of Clarion West, where he studied under the likes of Chuck Palahniuk, Connie Willis, and Cory Doctorow.

He lives in Portland, OR, the bizarro fiction mecca.

Visit him online at **www.carltonmellick.com**

BIZARRO BOOKS

CATALOG   FALL 2011

ERASERHEAD PRESS

Your major resource for the bizarro fiction genre:

WWW.BIZARROCENTRAL.COM

Introduce yourselves to the bizarro fiction genre and all of its authors with the Bizarro Starter Kit series. Each volume features short novels and short stories by ten of the leading bizarro authors, designed to give you a perfect sampling of the genre for only $10.

BB-0X1
"The Bizarro Starter Kit"
(Orange)
Featuring D. Harlan Wilson, Carlton Mellick III, Jeremy Robert Johnson, Kevin L Donihe, Gina Ranalli, Andre Duza, Vincent W. Sakowski, Steve Beard, John Edward Lawson, and Bruce Taylor. **236 pages $10**

BB-0X2
"The Bizarro Starter Kit"
(Blue)
Featuring Ray Fracalossy, Jeremy C. Shipp, Jordan Krall, Mykle Hansen, Andersen Prunty, Eckhard Gerdes, Bradley Sands, Steve Aylett, Christian TeBordo, and Tony Rauch. **244 pages $10**

BB-0X2
"The Bizarro Starter Kit"
(Purple)
Featuring Russell Edson, Athena Villaverde, David Agranoff, Matthew Revert, Andrew Goldfarb, Jeff Burk, Garrett Cook, Kris Saknussemm, Cody Goodfellow, and Cameron Pierce **264 pages $10**

BB-001 **"The Kafka Effekt" D. Harlan Wilson** — A collection of forty-four irreal short stories loosely written in the vein of Franz Kafka, with more than a pinch of William S. Burroughs sprinkled on top. **211 pages $14**

BB-002 **"Satan Burger" Carlton Mellick III** — The cult novel that put Carlton Mellick III on the map ... Six punks get jobs at a fast food restaurant owned by the devil in a city violently overpopulated by surreal alien cultures. **236 pages $14**

BB-003 **"Some Things Are Better Left Unplugged" Vincent Sakwoski** — Join The Man and his Nemesis, the obese tabby, for a nightmare roller coaster ride into this postmodern fantasy. **152 pages $10**

BB-004 **"Shall We Gather At the Garden?" Kevin L Donihe** — Donihe's Debut novel. Midgets take over the world, The Church of Lionel Richie vs. The Church of the Byrds, plant porn and more! **244 pages $14**

BB-005 **"Razor Wire Pubic Hair" Carlton Mellick III** — A genderless humandildo is purchased by a razor dominatrix and brought into her nightmarish world of bizarre sex and mutilation. **176 pages $11**

BB-006 **"Stranger on the Loose" D. Harlan Wilson** — The fiction of Wilson's 2nd collection is planted in the soil of normalcy, but what grows out of that soil is a dark, witty, otherworldly jungle... **228 pages $14**

BB-007 **"The Baby Jesus Butt Plug" Carlton Mellick III** — Using clones of the Baby Jesus for anal sex will be the hip sex fetish of the future. **92 pages $10**

BB-008 **"Fishyfleshed" Carlton Mellick III** — The world of the past is an illogical flatland lacking in dimension and color, a sick-scape of crispy squid people wandering the desert for no apparent reason. **260 pages $14**

BB-009 **"Dead Bitch Army" Andre Duza** — Step into a world filled with racist teenagers, cannibals, 100 warped Uncle Sams, automobiles with razor-sharp teeth, living graffiti, and a pissed-off zombie bitch out for revenge. **344 pages $16**

BB-010 **"The Menstruating Mall" Carlton Mellick III** — "The Breakfast Club meets Chopping Mall as directed by David Lynch." - Brian Keene **212 pages $12**

BB-011 **"Angel Dust Apocalypse" Jeremy Robert Johnson** — Meth-heads, man-made monsters, and murderous Neo-Nazis. "Seriously amazing short stories..." - Chuck Palahniuk, author of Fight Club **184 pages $11**

BB-012 **"Ocean of Lard" Kevin L Donihe / Carlton Mellick III** — A parody of those old Choose Your Own Adventure kid's books about some very odd pirates sailing on a sea made of animal fat. **176 pages $12**

BB-015 **"Foop!" Chris Genoa** — Strange happenings are going on at Dactyl, Inc, the world's first and only time travel tourism company.
"A surreal pie in the face!" - Christopher Moore **300 pages $14**

BB-020 **"Punk Land" Carlton Mellick III** — In the punk version of Heaven, the anarchist utopia is threatened by corporate fascism and only Goblin, Mortician's sperm, and a blue-mohawked female assassin named Shark Girl can stop them. **284 pages $15**

BB-027 **"Siren Promised" Jeremy Robert Johnson & Alan M Clark** — Nominated for the Bram Stoker Award. A potent mix of bad drugs, bad dreams, brutal bad guys, and surreal/incredible art by Alan M. Clark. **190 pages $13**

BB-031 **"Sea of the Patchwork Cats" Carlton Mellick III** — A quiet dreamlike tale set in the ashes of the human race. For Mellick enthusiasts who also adore The Twilight Zone. **112 pages $10**

BB-032 "Extinction Journals" Jeremy Robert Johnson — An uncanny voyage across a newly nuclear America where one man must confront the problems associated with loneliness, insane dieties, radiation, love, and an ever-evolving cockroach suit with a mind of its own. **104 pages $10**

BB-037 "The Haunted Vagina" Carlton Mellick III — It's difficult to love a woman whose vagina is a gateway to the world of the dead. **132 pages $10**

BB-043 "War Slut" Carlton Mellick III — Part "1984," part "Waiting for Godot," and part action horror video game adaptation of John Carpenter's "The Thing." **116 pages $10**

BB-047 "Sausagey Santa" Carlton Mellick III — A bizarro Christmas tale featuring Santa as a piratey mutant with a body made of sausages. 124 pages $10

BB-048 "Misadventures in a Thumbnail Universe" Vincent Sakowski — Dive deep into the surreal and satirical realms of neo-classical Blender Fiction, filled with television shoes and flesh-filled skies. **120 pages $10**

BB-053 "Ballad of a Slow Poisoner" Andrew Goldfarb — Millford Mutterwurst sat down on a Tuesday to take his afternoon tea, and made the unpleasant discovery that his elbows were becoming flatter. **128 pages $10**

BB-055 "Help! A Bear is Eating Me" Mykle Hansen — The bizarro, heartwarming, magical tale of poor planning, hubris and severe blood loss...
150 pages $11

BB-056 "Piecemeal June" Jordan Krall — A man falls in love with a living sex doll, but with love comes danger when her creator comes after her with crab-squid assassins. **90 pages $9**

BB-058 "The Overwhelming Urge" Andersen Prunty — A collection of bizarro tales by Andersen Prunty. **150 pages $11**

BB-059 "Adolf in Wonderland" Carlton Mellick III — A dreamlike adventure that takes a young descendant of Adolf Hitler's design and sends him down the rabbit hole into a world of imperfection and disorder. **180 pages $11**

BB-061 "Ultra Fuckers" Carlton Mellick III — Absurdist suburban horror about a couple who enter an upper middle class gated community but can't find their way out. **108 pages $9**

BB-062 "House of Houses" Kevin L. Donihe — An odd man wants to marry his house. Unfortunately, all of the houses in the world collapse at the same time in the Great House Holocaust. Now he must travel to House Heaven to find his departed fiancee. **172 pages $11**

BB-064 "Squid Pulp Blues" Jordan Krall — In these three bizarro-noir novellas, the reader is thrown into a world of murderers, drugs made from squid parts, deformed gun-toting veterans, and a mischievous apocalyptic donkey. **204 pages $12**

BB-065 "Jack and Mr. Grin" Andersen Prunty — "When Mr. Grin calls you can hear a smile in his voice. Not a warm and friendly smile, but the kind that seizes your spine in fear. You don't need to pay your phone bill to hear it. That smile is in every line of Prunty's prose." - Tom Bradley. **208 pages $12**

BB-066 "Cybernetrix" Carlton Mellick III — What would you do if your normal everyday world was slowly mutating into the video game world from Tron? **212 pages $12**

BB-072 "Zerostrata" Andersen Prunty — Hansel Nothing lives in a tree house, suffers from memory loss, has a very eccentric family, and falls in love with a woman who runs naked through the woods every night. **144 pages $11**

BB-073 "The Egg Man" Carlton Mellick III — It is a world where humans reproduce like insects. Children are the property of corporations, and having an enormous ten-foot brain implanted into your skull is a grotesque sexual fetish. Mellick's industrial urban dystopia is one of his darkest and grittiest to date. **184 pages $11**

BB-074 "Shark Hunting in Paradise Garden" Cameron Pierce — A group of strange humanoid religious fanatics travel back in time to the Garden of Eden to discover it is invested with hundreds of giant flying maneating sharks. **150 pages $10**

BB-075 "Apeshit" Carlton Mellick III - Friday the 13th meets Visitor Q. Six hipster teens go to a cabin in the woods inhabited by a deformed killer. An incredibly fucked-up parody of B-horror movies with a bizarro slant. **192 pages $12**

BB-076 "Fuckers of Everything on the Crazy Shitting Planet of the Vomit At smosphere" Mykle Hansen - Three bizarro satires. Monster Cocks, Journey to the Center of Agnes Cuddlebottom, and Crazy Shitting Planet. **228 pages $12**

BB-077 "The Kissing Bug" Daniel Scott Buck — In the tradition of Roald Dahl, Tim Burton, and Edward Gorey, comes this bizarro anti-war children's story about a bohemian conenose kissing bug who falls in love with a human woman. **116 pages $10**

BB-078 "MachoPoni" Lotus Rose — It's My Little Pony... *Bizarro* style! A long time ago Poniworld was split in two. On one side of the Jagged Line is the Pastel Kingdom, a magical land of music, parties, and positivity. On the other side of the Jagged Line is Dark Kingdom inhabited by an army of undead ponies. **148 pages $11**

BB-079 "The Faggiest Vampire" Carlton Mellick III — A Roald Dahl-esque children's story about two faggy vampires who partake in a mustache competition to find out which one is truly the faggiest. **104 pages $10**

BB-080 "Sky Tongues" Gina Ranalli — The autobiography of Sky Tongues, the biracial hermaphrodite actress with tongues for fingers. Follow her strange life story as she rises from freak to fame. **204 pages $12**

BB-081 **"Washer Mouth" Kevin L. Donihe** - A washing machine becomes human and pursues his dream of meeting his favorite soap opera star. **244 pages $11**

BB-082 **"Shatnerquake" Jeff Burk** - All of the characters ever played by William Shatner are suddenly sucked into our world. Their mission: hunt down and destroy the real William Shatner. **100 pages $10**

BB-083 **"The Cannibals of Candyland" Carlton Mellick III** - There exists a race of cannibals that are made of candy. They live in an underground world made out of candy. One man has dedicated his life to killing them all. **170 pages $11**

BB-084 **"Slub Glub in the Weird World of the Weeping Willows"** **Andrew Goldfarb** - The charming tale of a blue glob named Slub Glub who helps the weeping willows whose tears are flooding the earth. There are also hyenas, ghosts, and a voodoo priest **100 pages $10**

BB-085 **"Super Fetus" Adam Pepper** - Try to abort this fetus and he'll kick your ass! **104 pages $10**

BB-086 **"Fistful of Feet" Jordan Krall** - A bizarro tribute to spaghetti westerns, featuring Cthulhu-worshipping Indians, a woman with four feet, a crazed gunman who is obsessed with sucking on candy, Syphilis-ridden mutants, sexually transmitted tattoos, and a house devoted to the freakiest fetishes. **228 pages $12**

BB-087 **"Ass Goblins of Auschwitz" Cameron Pierce** - It's Monty Python meets Nazi exploitation in a surreal nightmare as can only be imagined by Bizarro author Cameron Pierce. **104 pages $10**

BB-088 **"Silent Weapons for Quiet Wars" Cody Goodfellow** - "This is high-end psychological surrealist horror meets bottom-feeding low-life crime in a techno-thrilling science fiction world full of Lovecraft and magic..." -John Skipp **212 pages $12**

BB-089 **"Warrior Wolf Women of the Wasteland" Carlton Mellick III**
— Road Warrior Werewolves versus McDonaldland Mutants...post-apocalyptic fiction has never been quite like this. **316 pages $13**

BB-091 **"Super Giant Monster Time" Jeff Burk** — A tribute to choose your own adventures and Godzilla movies. Will you escape the giant monsters that are rampaging the fuck out of your city and shit? Or will you join the mob of alien-controlled punk rockers causing chaos in the streets? What happens next depends on you. **188 pages $12**

BB-092 **"Perfect Union" Cody Goodfellow** — "Cronenberg's THE FLY on a grand scale: human/insect gene-spliced body horror, where the human hive politics are as shocking as the gore." -John Skipp. **272 pages $13**

BB-093 **"Sunset with a Beard" Carlton Mellick III** — 14 stories of surreal science fiction. **200 pages $12**

BB-094 **"My Fake War" Andersen Prunty** — The absurd tale of an unlikely soldier forced to fight a war that, quite possibly, does not exist. It's Rambo meets Waiting for Godot in this subversive satire of American values and the scope of the human imagination. **128 pages $11**

BB-095 **"Lost in Cat Brain Land" Cameron Pierce** — Sad stories from a surreal world. A fascist mustache, the ghost of Franz Kafka, a desert inside a dead cat. Primordial entities mourn the death of their child. The desperate serve tea to mysterious creatures. A hopeless romantic falls in love with a pterodactyl. And much more. **152 pages $11**

BB-096 **"The Kobold Wizard's Dildo of Enlightenment +2" Carlton Mellick III** — A Dungeons and Dragons parody about a group of people who learn they are only made up characters in an AD&D campaign and must find a way to resist their nerdy teenaged players and retarded dungeon master in order to survive. 232 **pages $12**

BB-098 **"A Hundred Horrible Sorrows of Ogner Stump" Andrew Goldfarb** — Goldfarb's acclaimed comic series. A magical and weird journey into the horrors of everyday life. **164 pages $11**

BB-099 "Pickled Apocalypse of Pancake Island" Cameron Pierce—A
demented fairy tale about a pickle, a pancake, and the apocalypse. **102 pages $8**

BB-100 "Slag Attack" Andersen Prunty— Slag Attack features four visceral,
noir stories about the living, crawling apocalypse. A slag is what survivors are calling the
slug-like maggots raining from the sky, burrowing inside people, and hollowing out their
flesh and their sanity. **148 pages $11**

BB-101 "Slaughterhouse High" Robert Devereaux—A place where
schools are built with secret passageways, rebellious teens get zippers installed in their
mouths and genitals, and once a year, on that special night, one couple is slaughtered and
the bits of their bodies are kept as souvenirs. **304 pages $13**

BB-102 "The Emerald Burrito of Oz" John Skipp & Marc Levinthal
—OZ IS REAL! Magic is real! The gate is really in Kansas! And America is finally allowing
Earth tourists to visit this weird-ass, mysterious land. But when Gene of Los Angeles heads off
for summer vacation in the Emerald City, little does he know that a war is brewing...a war that
could destroy both worlds. **280 pages $13**

BB-103 "The Vegan Revolution... with Zombies" David Agranoff —
When there's no more meat in hell, the vegans will walk the earth. **160 pages $11**

BB-104 "The Flappy Parts" Kevin L Donihe—Poems about bunnies, LSD,
and police abuse. You know, things that matter. 132 **pages $11**

BB-105 "Sorry I Ruined Your Orgy" Bradley Sands—Bizarro humorist
Bradley Sands returns with one of the strangest, most hilarious collections of the year. **130
pages $11**

BB-106 "Mr. Magic Realism" Bruce Taylor—Like Golden Age science fic-
tion comics written by Freud, *Mr. Magic Realism* is a strange, insightful adventure that
spans the furthest reaches of the galaxy, exploring the hidden caverns in the hearts and
minds of men, women, aliens, and biomechanical cats. **152 pages $11**

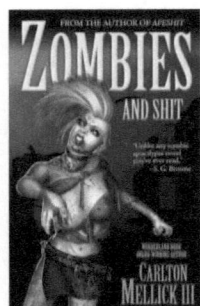   

BB-107 **"Zombies and Shit" Carlton Mellick III**—"Battle Royale" meets "Return of the Living Dead." Mellick's bizarro tribute to the zombie genre. **308 pages $13**

BB-108 **"The Cannibal's Guide to Ethical Living" Mykle Hansen**—Over a five star French meal of fine wine, organic vegetables and human flesh, a lunatic delivers a witty, chilling, disturbingly sane argument in favor of eating the rich.. **184 pages $11**

BB-109 **"Starfish Girl" Athena Villaverde**—In a post-apocalyptic underwater dome society, a girl with a starfish growing from her head and an assassin with sea anenome hair are on the run from a gang of mutant fish men. **160 pages $11**

BB-110 **"Lick Your Neighbor" Chris Genoa**—Mutant ninjas, a talking whale, kung fu masters, maniacal pilgrims, and an alcoholic clown populate Chris Genoa's surreal, darkly comical and unnerving reimagining of the first Thanksgiving. **303 pages $13**

BB-111 **"Night of the Assholes" Kevin L. Donihe**—A plague of assholes is infecting the countryside. Normal everyday people are transforming into jerks, snobs, dicks, and douchebags. And they all have only one purpose: to make your life a living hell.. **192 pages $11**

BB-112 **"Jimmy Plush, Teddy Bear Detective" Garrett Cook**—Hardboiled cases of a private detective trapped within a teddy bear body. **180 pages $11**

BB-113 **"The Deadheart Shelters" Forrest Armstrong**—The hip hop lovechild of William Burroughs and Dali... **144 pages $11**

BB-114 **"Eyeballs Growing All Over Me... Again" Tony Raugh**—Absurd, surreal, playful, dream-like, whimsical, and a lot of fun to read. **144 pages $11**

BB-115 **"Whargoul" Dave Brockie** — From the killing grounds of Stalingrad to the death camps of the holocaust. From torture chambers in Iraq to race riots in the United States, the Whargoul was there, killing and raping. **244 pages $12**

BB-116 **"By the Time We Leave Here, We'll Be Friends" J. David Osborne** — A David Lynchian nightmare set in a Russian gulag, where its prisoners, guards, traitors, soldiers, lovers, and demons fight for survival and their own rapidly deteriorating humanity. **168 pages $11**

BB-117 **"Christmas on Crack" edited by Carlton Mellick III** — Perverted Christmas Tales for the whole family! . . . as long as every member of your family is over the age of 18. **168 pages $11**

BB-118 **"Crab Town" Carlton Mellick III** — Radiation fetishists, balloon people, mutant crabs, sail-bike road warriors, and a love affair between a woman and an H-Bomb. This is one mean asshole of a city. Welcome to Crab Town. **100 pages $8**

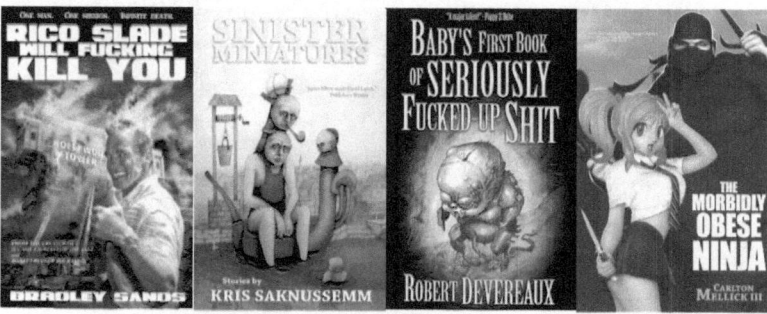

BB-119 **"Rico Slade Will Fucking Kill You" Bradley Sands** — Rico Slade is an action hero. Rico Slade can rip out a throat with his bare hands. Rico Slade's favorite food is the honey-roasted peanut. Rico Slade will fucking kill everyone. A novel. **122 pages $8**

BB-120 **"Sinister Miniatures" Kris Saknussemm** — The definitive collection of short fiction by Kris Saknussemm, confirming that he is one of the best, most daring writers of the weird to emerge in the twenty-first century. **180 pages $11**

BB-121 **"Baby's First Book of Seriously Fucked up Shit" Robert Devereaux** — Ten stories of the strange, the gross, and the just plain fucked up from one of the most original voices in horror. **176 pages $11**

BB-122 **"The Morbidly Obese Ninja" Carlton Mellick III** — These days, if you want to run a successful company . . . you're going to need a lot of ninjas. **92 pages $8**

BB-123 **"Abortion Arcade" Cameron Pierce** — An intoxicating blend of body horror and midnight movie madness, reminiscent of early David Lynch and the splatterpunks at their most sublime. **172 pages $11**

BB-124 **"Black Hole Blues" Patrick Wensink** — A hilarious double helix of country music and physics. **196 pages $11**

BB-125 **"Barbarian Beast Bitches of the Badlands" Carlton Mellick III** — Three prequels and sequels to *Warrior Wolf Women of the Wasteland*. **284 pages $13**

BB-126 **"The Traveling Dildo Salesman" Kevin L. Donihe** — A nightmare comedy about destiny, faith, and sex toys. Also featuring Donihe's most lurid and infamous short stories: *Milky Agitation, Two-Way Santa, The Helen Mower, Living Room Zombies,* and *Revenge of the Living Masturbation Rag.* **108 pages $8**

BB-127 **"Metamorphosis Blues" Bruce Taylor** — Enter a land of love beasts, intergalactic cowboys, and rock 'n roll. A land where Sears Catalogs are doorways to insanity and men keep mysterious black boxes. Welcome to the monstrous mind of Mr. Magic Realism. **136 pages $11**

BB-128 **"The Driver's Guide to Hitting Pedestrians" Andersen Prunty** — A pocket guide to the twenty-three most painful things in life, written by the most well-adjusted man in the universe. **108 pages $8**

BB-129 **"Island of the Super People" Kevin Shamel** — Four students and their anthropology professor journey to a remote island to study its indigenous population. But this is no ordinary native culture. They're super heroes and villains with flesh costumes and outlandish abilities like self-detonation, musical eyelashes, and microwave hands. **194 pages $11**

BB-130 **"Fantastic Orgy" Carlton Mellick III** — Shark Sex, mutant cats, and strange sexually transmitted diseases. Featuring the stories: *Candy-coated, Ear Cat, Fantastic Orgy, City Hobgoblins,* and *Porno in August.* **136 pages $9**

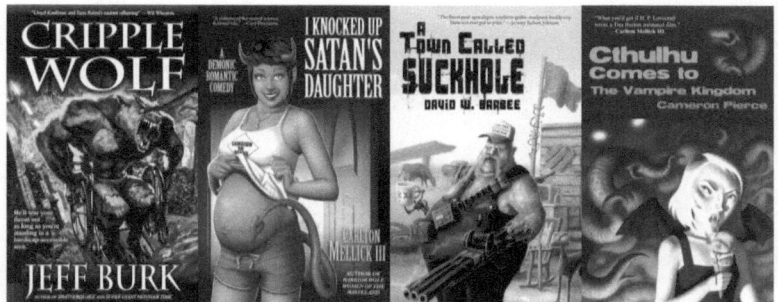

BB-131 **"Cripple Wolf" Jeff Burk** — Part man. Part wolf. 100% crippled. Also including *Punk Rock Nursing Home, Adrift with Space Badgers, Cook for Your Life, Just Another Day in the Park, Frosty and the Full Monty,* and *House of Cats.* **152 pages $10**

BB-132 **"I Knocked Up Satan's Daughter" Carlton Mellick III** — An adorable, violent, fantastical love story. A romantic comedy for the bizarro fiction reader. **152 pages $10**

BB-133 **"A Town Called Suckhole" David W. Barbee** — Far into the future, in the nuclear bowels of post-apocalyptic Dixie, there is a town. A town of derelict mobile homes, ancient junk, and mutant wildlife. A town of slack jawed rednecks who bask in the splendors of moonshine and mud boggin'. A town dedicated to the bloody and demented legacy of the Old South. A town called Suckhole. **144 pages $10**

BB-134 **"Cthulhu Comes to the Vampire Kingdom" Cameron Pierce** — What you'd get if H. P. Lovecraft wrote a Tim Burton animated film. **148 pages $11**

BB-135 **"I am Genghis Cum" Violet LeVoit** — From the savage Arctic tundra to post-partum mutations to your missing daughter's unmarked grave, join visionary madwoman Violet LeVoit in this non-stop eight-story onslaught of full-tilt Bizarro punk lit thrills. **124 pages $9**

BB-136 **"Haunt" Laura Lee Bahr** — A tripping-balls Los Angeles noir, where a mysterious dame drags you through a time-warping Bizarro hall of mirrors. **316 pages $13**

BB-137 **"Amazing Stories of the Flying Spaghetti Monster" edited by Cameron Pierce** — Like an all-spaghetti evening of Adult Swim, the Flying Spaghetti Monster will show you the many realms of His Noodly Appendage. Learn of those who worship him and the lives he touches in distant, mysterious ways. **228 pages $12**

BB-138 **"Wave of Mutilation" Douglas Lain** — A dream-pop exploration of modern architecture and the American identity, *Wave of Mutilation* is a Zen finger trap for the 21st century. **100 pages $8**